F1421

The Media
Good

D1428032

The Media Crew 1
Good News/
Bad News

Stephen Rabley

An Arma

First published in Armada in 1989

Armada is an imprint of the
Children's Division of the
Collins Publishing Group
8 Grafton Street, London W1X 3LA

Copyright © Stephen Rabley 1989

Printed in Great Britain by
William Collins Sons & Co. Ltd, Glasgow

Chapter 1

Jake Shepherd sat completely motionless in the blue armchair. On a portable TV at his feet Wilma Flintstone was making omelettes with pterodactyl eggs. Jake smiled, then sneaked a glance at his watch. "Mum," he muttered, "– it's nearly six and you haven't even changed yet."

No reply.

"Mum?"

"Nearly finished," came an absorbed voice from across the chaotic, sunlit studio. For a moment there was nothing but a mixture of cartoon sound effects and distant traffic noise from Notting Hill Gate, then the voice resumed. "I'm just doing your chin, all right? – so don't move a muscle for the next two minutes."

Jake sighed. Perfect. Now they were going to be late for the lower-sixth parents "do" at Portobello because of his chin. Groaning inwardly he began watching television again, deftly turning the sound up with a socked foot as the six o'clock news came on. A bomb in Paris, the unemployment figures, a plane crash in Brazil, clips of a parliamentary debate, the F. T. Index, Charles and Diana at a film première – one by one the main stories flashed onto the screen accompanied by slick computer graphics and a stern voice-over.

"Doom, gloom and royals," said Kay Shepherd, squinting abstractedly at her canvas. "Is that really all that goes on in the world?" She stepped back and ran one hand down her paint-spattered smock. "There. That's it for today. Want to have a look?"

Jake stretched with noisy relief and reached for the OFF button as his mother turned the easel round. Well, it was starting to look like him all right – even he could see the likeness now. She'd got the barber-proof blond cowlick, the angular, foxy outline of his face, the long fingers, rangy build, even the rip in one knee of his faded 501s. "Yeah – it's really coming on," he said appreciatively. Kay smiled vaguely and made an adjustment to her unruly, pinned-up hair.

"Mmmm," she half agreed. "There's something not quite right about the eyes, though." Jake helpfully went cross-eyed and got a playful raised hand in response. "No, idiot – I mean not enough expression. After all, the eyes are supposed to be 'the windows of the soul'. Who said that? Was it Shelley?" She frowned, turning momentarily into an older, slightly less pretty version of Felicity Kendal. "No, it couldn't have been – it was earlier than Shelley. Could even have bee . . ."

"Mum." Jake pointed to his watch. "I said we'd pick Mojo up at quarter past."

"Hmmm? Oh yes, of course. I'd better go and get changed, hadn't I?" Jake nodded slowly as his mother patted him on the cheek, walked out and clattered up the uncarpeted stairs. "How come I always have to be the responsible one round here?" he murmured to a silver-framed photograph of his father on the mantelpiece. Then, with a rueful shake of the head, he bent down to retrieve his shoes from under the blue armchair.

Five minutes later, Kay Shepherd's ancient pink 2CV pulled up outside a three-storey terraced house in Ladbroke Grove. Jamaican reggae was pulsing out of an upstairs window and a small girl with plaits was giant-stepping round the pocket-handkerchief front garden with a doll firmly gripped under one arm. Jake got out of the car and ran up the front path.

"Hi, Phoebe," he called. "Do you know where your brother is?" The little girl stopped her game and broke into a broad grin, revealing a large gap where her front teeth should have been. She pointed at an open upstairs window.

"He's in his room," she announced slowly and deliberately. "*Dan*-cing." She wiggled her bottom by way of demonstration as the music stopped and a beaming face emerged at the window. Jake looked up, shielding his eyes against the fading, early September sun.

"Ready to go?" he shouted.

"Yep," came the reply. "Ready and waiting."

By the time Jake had got back into the car, Mojo Johnson was jogging down the path dressed in a lemon-yellow shirt, black slacks and a pair of topsiders.

"Hi, Mrs Shepherd," he said to Kay as he wedged himself into the back seat.

"Hello, Maurice," she replied. "Sorry we're late. Domestic chaos as usual, I'm afraid." Jake turned round and gave his friend a knowing look.

"No problem," grinned Mojo affably, then reached out a hand to steady himself as the 2CV drove jerkily away.

"Let's see if I've got this straight," said Kay a few seconds later. "The point of this evening is for everyone to meet before the new term begins. The head gives a speech, then we all mill around nibbling little eats on sticks and being sociable. Am I right?"

"I dunno," said Mojo. "I just hope it's over by nine, that's all. QPR are on the telly tonight." There was a moment's pause before Jake, who was looking out of the window, inhaled audibly.

"Portobello Sixth Form College," he mused. "I still can't believe we're not going back to St Mary Abbott's next week." He looked over his shoulder at Mojo. "You know what I mean?"

Mojo nodded. "It's the dawning of a new era," he intoned in his Hollywood newsreel voice.

Jake smiled. "Well it is . . . in a way."

7

The car park at Portobello College seemed completely full at twenty-five past six. Finding a place wasn't going to be easy, and as the 2CV drove up and down for the second time Jake felt a knot of anxiety and excitement being tied in his stomach. He was going to spend a lot of time here in the next two years. Then he became aware of something else – it was a finger jabbing insistently at his left shoulder. He turned and saw Mojo pointing to a large silver BMW parked just ahead of them. An expensive-looking middle-aged couple were sitting in the front, but that wasn't the reason for Mojo's interest. Stepping out of the back seat was a girl of sixteen or seventeen with waist-length auburn hair, an ivory-coloured silk blouse and designer jeans. Jake watched her push a lock of stray hair gracefully over one shoulder then turn and look round. For a fraction of a second her eyes registered the 2CV and Jake was sure he noticed a tiny smile form at the corners of her mouth.

"Check . . . it . . . out," whispered Mojo, wiggling both eyebrows lasciviously. Jake shook his head in total disbelief.

"Johnson! We haven't even got through the front door. Control yourself!" He paused, still looking at the BMW girl, who was now walking away from the car with the middle-aged couple – presumably her parents. "Anyway," he went on more calmly, "she looks totally stuck-up to me. A real rich bi — "

"When you two have *quite* finished with the sexist remarks . . ." said Kay, turning into a newly-vacated parking space and putting on the handbrake.

"Sorry, Mrs Shepherd," grinned Mojo apologetically.

Kay turned to her son. "Well, don't look at me!" Jake protested. "*He* started it!"

Inside the school's airy, modern-looking hall, an audience of about three hundred had already gathered. People were gazing about, waving to each other, taking off their coats and producing the general buzz of conversation which Jake always thought of as "crowd speak". He took in the overall scene, including several familiar faces from St Mary Abbott's, then turned his attention to the stage. On it there was a lectern and behind the lectern sat a line of idly-chatting men and women who could only be the staff of the college.

Just at that moment an extremely tall man in a blue suit walked on stage, striding purposefully towards the lectern. He was at least six foot four, with iron-grey hair and the face of a harassed Roman senator. Quickly the Shepherds and Mojo found three seats at the back of the hall and had barely sat down before the man began to speak.

"Good evening, everyone." He had a Yorkshire accent. "It's just gone six-thirty, so if we can begin . . ." A residual hum of conversation from the body of the hall gradually faded into silence. "Thank you." The man cleared his throat and placed one hand between the second and third buttons of his jacket. "Now, my name is Tom Busby and as the headmaster of Portobello Sixth Form College it's my pleasure and privilege to welcome you all here this evening. As you know the purpose of this event is to give our new intake of students the chance to look round and get acquainted with the staff before term starts next week. It's also, of course, a chance for us to have an early look at *you*!" He paused expectantly while a polite ripple of laughter floated round the hall and rapidly died.

"But before we get down to the main business of the evening, I'd like if I may to say a few words about the school itself."

For the next twenty minutes Tom Busby gave a glowing account of the school's history, academic record and its plans for dealing with what he called "the present education revolution". Meanwhile Mojo, watched out of one eye by Jake, gradually slumped lower and lower into his seat. Finally, though, the headmaster reached the end of his address.

". . . so all that remains is for me to point out the refreshment tables at the back of the hall and draw your attention to the name and subject tags which my colleagues" – with an expansive gesture he indicated the line of teachers behind him – "are wearing for ease of identification. I hope you find the rest of the evening informative and enjoyable. Thank you."

"Well, he's a barrel of laughs and no mistake," said Mojo grimly, as everyone stood up and began moving towards the back of the hall.

"I shouldn't think we'll have much to do with him," replied Jake. "Anyway, he seemed harmless enough to me."

"Yeah – as long as you're not afraid of death by boredom."

"Maurice!" said Kay, smiling in spite of herself. She turned to Jake. "Have *you* got that letter they sent with the names of all the teachers, or did you give it to me?"

Jake fished in the pocket of his baseball jacket and pulled out a crumpled piece of paper. "It's here," he said, "OK – our mission is to find Cora Peters: A level English, Adrian Brand: A level Music, and Phil Hammond: GCSE Media Studies."

"And I . . ." Mojo theatrically produced a similar wrinkled sheet ". . . Yeah, I'm after Brand and Hammond, too, plus some guy called Barry Crane who's got me in his computer studies class."

"Right," said Kay. "What I suggest is this. Coffee first, then we split up – you find your Mr Crane, we'll find . . ." she looked at Jake's list "Cora Peters, then we'll meet up here again and track down the other two. Agreed?"

"Faultless logic, Mrs Shepherd," said Mojo. "Completely faultless."

Forty minutes later Adrian Brand, a tall, distinguished-looking man of about sixty, offered a dead-fish handshake to Kay, Mojo and Jake. "Well, good to have met you all, and I look forward to seeing *you* two" (here he beamed unreservedly at the boys) "next week for our first formal academic encounter." With that he turned and left.

"What makes you think he's not a heavy metal fan?" said Mojo.

"Mmmm," Jake agreed. "But did you get the bit about the soundproof rehearsal room?"

"Too right I did!" Mojo grinned enthusiastically. "That's the first good news I've heard all night. We'll have a look at it on Monday, eh?"

Kay put down her coffee cup. "Right," she said. "One to go. The Media Studies man – what's his name?"

"Hammond," said Jake. "Phil Hammond."

The three of them spent several unsuccessful minutes looking for the relevant name tag, with Mojo getting more and more edgy as time went on. Finally he couldn't bear it any more. "Look," he blurted out. "Obviously the guy's not here, right – so what do you say we call it a day?" He glanced at his watch. "I mean, I know school's important and all that, but let's face facts – the QPR match begins in twenty minutes. It's a question of priorities – know what I mean?"

Kay put a hand on his shoulder. "Maurice – let me ask *you* a question. Do you know what 'in loco parentis' means?" Mojo shook his head very slowly. "Well," Kay went on, "it means that since your Mum and Dad are on holiday in Trinidad, and since they asked me to make sure you came tonight and met *all* your teachers, I don't think . . ."

Mojo held up his hands. "OK, OK, I get the drift, Mrs Shepherd." He sighed morosely. "All I'm saying is I wish this idiot Hammond would show up soon, that's all."

"Well, here he is," said a voice. Mojo spun round and found himself staring straight at the lapel of a leather jacket. On it was a name tag bearing the words PHIL HAMMOND – MEDIA STUDIES. He gave a barely audible groan.

11

"Oh, Mr Hammond, we were just looking for you," said Kay, brightly. "My name's Kay Shepherd. This is my son Jake and his friend, Maurice Johnson. They're both going to be in your group."

Phil Hammond smiled and nodded. He had rumpled, sandy hair, pale skin and amused, deep-set eyes. There was an oil stain on the collar of his shirt. "Sorry I wasn't here earlier," he said, "but my motor-bike broke down – second time this week. Anyway, I've heard Tom Busby's pre-term speech before, so it could have been worse. Look, why don't we find somewhere a bit quieter?"

They settled themselves at a corner table, then Phil Hammond took a slim folder out of his briefcase. "Well, basically, GCSE Media Studies is a very practical one-year course," he began. "There's a certain amount of straight-forward syllabus bumpf to get through – that goes without saying," he pointed at the folder, "but I try to leave as much time as possible for project work."

"Sounds good," said Jake. "You mean making videos – that sort of thing?"

"Hmmm." Phil took off his jacket. "And writing soap-opera scripts, visiting radio stations, putting together photo-stories. You see, each term is based round a theme. The first one is the written word – newspapers, magazines, and so on. Then you get 'sound' – that's radio and the music industry."

"The music industry?" said Mojo, brightening considerably. "Great! See, Jake and me are thinking of starting a band."

Phil spread his hands. "That's ideal. Maybe you'll be able to do something on the pop press, or how studios work, or the way record companies treat young bands."

"What happens in the third term?" asked Jake.

"Hang on," said Phil and riffled through the folder. "This year the third term is . . . oh, of course, 'the visual media' – TV, video and film."

"And all this practical work counts towards the GCSE

itself, does it?" asked Kay, with a note of amazed belief.

"Oh yes," replied Phil. "In fact it *is* the GCSE. 100% of the marks come from coursework and projects – there's no exam."

"Bit different from when you were at school, eh Mum?" said Jake.

"You're not kidding," answered Kay. "It sounds like you two are going to have a very good time. In fact . . ." she gave Phil Hammond a questioning glance ". . . you wouldn't have any spare places for mature students, would you?" Phil laughed, then raised an acknowledging hand to someone on the other side of the hall. It was Tom Busby, who looked less than amused and was making agitated beckoning signs.

"If you'll excuse me," said Phil. "I think my late arrival's just been noticed by Uncle Tom."

Jake looked across the room. "Is that what you call him?"

"Among other things," replied Phil. "See you next week, eh?"

"Yeah," said Jake. "See you next week."

Mojo and the Shepherds were just about to leave when Kay recognized someone.

"Good Lord, there's Gudrun Cormack. I haven't seen her for years!"

"Gudrun?" said Mojo. "There's a human being called 'Gudrun'?"

"Listen," Kay went on. "I'll just go over and say 'hello'. Shan't be long, I promise."

As she disappeared into the crowd, Mojo looked anxiously at his watch again. "I'm gonna catch the bus, OK? I mean, 'I'll just go over and say hello' is ten minutes minimum, right?"

Jake grinned. "Right. Hey, that Hammond bloke seems OK, don't you think?"

"Yeah," Mojo reluctantly allowed. "A bit pleased with

13

himself, but . . . yeah . . . he might not turn out to be an idiot after all."

They both laughed, then Jake said: "I'll call you tomorrow. Why don't you come over in the afternoon and we'll do some practising?"

"OK," Mojo agreed, already moving towards the door. "Have fun," he called over his shoulder.

Left alone, Jake leaned against a pillar and scanned the crowd. It was beginning to thin out a bit now. "Which of this lot will I get to know over the next two years?" he wondered, looking round pensively. Then he saw his mother. She was standing with a group of three other people, signalling for him to come over. Only when he was halfway across the hall did Jake realize who the three people were. It was the BMW girl and her parents.

"Jake," said Kay. "This is Mr and Mrs Cormack and their daughter, Charlotte."

Jake shook hands with the parents and gave Charlotte a barely perceptible nod which she returned in kind. "Mrs Cormack and I knew each other ages ago at art school," Kay went on. "We were just saying, weren't we, it must be all of— "

"Eighteen years," said Gudrun Cormack in a "how awful!" voice. A short pause followed this information. In the middle of it Jake became aware that his mother was willing him, by a slight widening of her eyes, to make conversation with Charlotte. He cleared his throat. "So, er, where've you been going to school up till now, Charlotte?"

The BMW girl looked at him and Jake recognized the same tiny hint of a smile he'd noticed earlier in the car park. "I was at Dartington." Jake got the impression he was supposed to know where that was.

"Yes," interrupted Gudrun Cormack. "Then Antony's company decided they simply couldn't do without him here in London, so we moved up from Devon about six weeks ago. Of course we wanted Charlotte to go to another private school, but no," she straightened the lapel of her daughter's silk blouse, "she simply insisted on a state school – didn't you, darling? So, here we are."

Charlotte's father, who looked prosperous and bored in equal measure, tapped her on the shoulder at this point. "Why don't you and . . ." he looked at Jake.

"Jake," said Jake.

"Why don't you and Jake go and get us all some coffee?"

"Oh yes, do, darling," said Gudrun Cormack. "I'm simply parched. Anyway, Kay, as I was saying . . . this house we've found in Holland Park is perfectly sweet. It's in a little street called Briardale Crescent and you wouldn't believe how— "

Jake and Charlotte stood in silence beside one of the trestle tables at the back of the hall while she began filling cups from a slow-pouring metal urn and he put them on a tray. They were halfway through this process for the second time when she said: "Only my parents call me Charlotte. Most people call me Charlie."

"I see," said Jake. He thought for a moment. "And I suppose really close friends call you Chuck." This was supposed to be an ice-breaking joke, except Charlie didn't laugh. Instead she passed him the second cup with a long, expressionless stare which lasted for several seconds before turning suddenly, unexpectedly, into a social smile.

"Sorry, but I don't think I quite caught your name. Jack, was it?"

Jake shifted his weight from one leg to the other. "Jake, actually," he replied.

The dialogue stopped at this point while Charlie devoted her full attention to the third cup of coffee and Jake watched her with an amused expression. She might be stuck up, but there was something about her that wasn't totally unfancyable – he couldn't say what it was yet, but there was definitely something. "So how come you decided to go to a state school?" he eventually asked, taking the third cup. Charlie gave him a sidelong glance and apparently decided the question was genuine.

"Lots of reasons. I wanted to get away from the whole privilege thing – have an ordinary social life . . . you know."

"Well, I don't actually," replied Jake, "but I'll take your word for it. Next please."

"What?"

"Next cup."

"Oh, yes." Charlie began filling the fourth cup, then spoke again. "The other thing is we've got this American girl coming to live with us for a year."

"An American girl?"

"Hmmm. We used to live in California, you see."

"Oh. Right."

"And this friend of mine – Lauren – wrote to say that she's doing a year here at Portobello College on some exchange or other. Anyway, I talked Mummy and Daddy into letting her live with us, and I thought it would be fun if I came here, too." Charlie flicked the handle of the urn to OFF and passed Jake another cup of coffee for his growing collection. Then, as he took it, she moved her weight onto one hip and changed the subject. "I like your mother. She's very unstuffy, isn't she? Very relaxed."

Jake sniffed, repeating the word slowly in his mind. "R-e-l-a-x-e-d. Yeah, well I suppose that's one way of putting it."

"She said she's a painter," Charlie went on. "What kind of pictures does she do?"

Jake folded his arms and sniffed. "Portraits mostly – the house is full of them." An idea crossed his mind. At first he rejected it, then rejected his rejection. What the hell. "You should get her to ask you over – she loves showing them to people."

Charlie gave Jake's battered jacket and dishevelled

jeans a cool, calm appraisal before answering. "I'm afraid art's not really my strong point." She smiled sweetly. "My boyfriend likes it, though. In fact he's reading art history at Oxford."

Jake passed her an empty cup from the stack beside him. Well, that was clear enough, "Last one," he said. Then, leaning thoughtfully on the edge of the table he began to swing one leg in a random sort of way. OK – two could play at that game. "I bet he's the hearty type. In the rugby team – all that sort of stuff."

"Who?"

"Your art historian."

This remark visibly struck home in the form of a subtle but noticeable blush. "He's not *my* art historian, he's *an* art historian."

Jake chuckled.

"And what's that supposed to mean?" asked Charlie, narrowing her eyes.

It was Jake's turn to smile sweetly. "Nothing."

"Are you sure?"

"Quite sure." He coughed lightly. "I bet he's got a really 'hooray' name, too – something like Jasper or Sebastian."

The blush deepened. "Not that it's any of your business, but if you *must* know, his name happens to be Julian."

"Thought so."

Turning sideways on, Charlie delivered a ferociously straight look. "Are you implying that because he's called Julian he must automatically be some sort of upper class . . . upper class . . ." she struggled to find the right noun, ". . . *nerd?*" Because if you are . . ."

Jake raised one finger. "Sorry to interrupt, but you're about to spill coffee all over your hand."

Charlie had forgotten all about the cup she was holding and looked down just in time to see hot coffee overflowing onto her fingers. With one very brief, high-pitched scream, she jumped backwards and simultaneously threw

17

the cup away from her. Amazingly, not a single drop of its steaming, mud-coloured contents missed Jake. For a long moment he stood motionless, looking down at his dripping baseball jacket in stunned dismay. Then, calmly, patiently, he raised his eyes until they met Charlie's. She was standing with both hands covering her mouth, trying unsuccessfully not to laugh.

"Thanks," he finally managed to say, through gritted teeth.

"It was your fault!" Charlie protested. "You made me do it." Several people in the vicinity of the trestle table had turned round to see what was happening. One of them was Phil Hammond.

"Well," he remarked, picking up a handful of paper napkins from beside the urn and passing them to Jake. "All I can say is I hope you two get on a little better than this in the Media Studies group."

Jake looked at him, then at Charlie, then at Phil again. "You mean both of us are . . ." He groaned and closed his eyes. Partly as a reaction to what he'd just been told and partly because a rivulet of coffee had just found its way inside his jeans.

Chapter 2

As the nine o'clock bell stopped ringing, Cora Peters picked up her bag and gazed round the fast-emptying staffroom. Why, she wondered, did Monday mornings never, *never* get any easier? Rummaging in a drawer, she produced a bottle of multi-vitamin pills and popped one. Then, casting a tight-lipped smile towards Adrian Brand and Phil Hammond, she stood up and headed for the door.

"Right – that's the lot!" Adrian threw the essay he'd been marking onto a pile in his briefcase and shut the lid. "Coming?" Phil glanced up from the *Independent* and nodded.

As they walked out of the staffroom Adrian said, "Oh, I meant to ask – how's Sally? Can't be long now."

"No, it's not." Phil nervously adjusted the books he was holding. "Any day, in fact."

Watching Adrian and Phil leave. Tom Busby turned back to his deputy, Barry Crane. "I didn't know young Hammond's wife was expecting a baby," he remarked.

"So I believe," murmured Barry, pushing his gold-rimmed spectacles back into place with a stubby forefinger.

"Well, well, well," Tom beamed affably. He looked at his watch and began to move away, but felt a restraining hand on his sleeve.

"Oh, Headmaster, before you go . . ." Barry cleared his throat and glanced round the now deserted staffroom. "Those recommendations you asked me to draw up – you know, about the college's future staffing and financing situation?"

"Yes."

"They're ready."

Down the corridor in Room 28 Mojo was absently turning the pages of a tabloid newspaper while next to him Jake gazed into the middle distance with Walkman headphones clamped in place and both palms keeping time on the top of his desk. "Dear, oh dear, oh dear," said Mojo to no one in particular. His neighbour, Brendan Tolley, looked out from behind a copy of the *Financial Times*. He had short, well-brushed red hair and was wearing a knitted tie.

"Yes?" he enquired. Sucking air through his teeth, Mojo turned the newspaper so that Brendan could see.

"How *does* she stop herself falling over?" he asked. The photograph had a powerful and immediate effect on Brendan Tolley. His studious face flushed a vivid shade of pink and he began blinking vigorously.

"I'm afraid I have no idea," he replied.

Mojo grunted in agreement. "Me neither." He tapped Jake on the shoulder, eager to canvas another opinion.

"What?" asked Jake, slipping off his headphones. Mojo presented the relevant page. Jake sighed. "I'd seriously consider hormone treatment if I were you," he said. "Talk about a one-track mind."

"He's not looking at smutty pictures again, is he?" said a tall girl with close-cropped blonde hair who had just walked in. She was wearing a haughty expression, no make-up, a maroon smock dress and cowboy boots. "Let's see," she said, stalking across the room and snatching the paper out of Mojo's hands.

"Oi, Lindsey!" he complained. "I was looking at . . .!"

"Pathetic," said Lindsey Jordan. "I mean really pathetic. I've never seen anything less erotic in all my life."

"It's just a bit of fun," protested Mojo.

"*Fun!*" Lindsey installed herself purposefully at a desk in front of Mojo. "This isn't a bit of fun," she said, pointing at the grinning Page Three girl. "This is sexist, exploitative, mind-numbing . . ." she shook her head, unable to finish the sentence.

" 'Crap', is the word you're looking for," said Aftab Jehar from the other side of the room. Mojo gave him a withering look.

"No, it's *not*!" said Aftab's neighbour, who was short, tough-looking and had a peroxide crew-cut. "Mojo's right. It's just a laugh, that's all. Giving the people what they want."

"Thank you, Dave," replied Mojo with relief. "I'm glad somebody round here agrees with me." Dave Anderson nodded his peroxide crew-cut in earnest support.

"Brendan?" asked Mojo. "Where do you stand on this?" Brendan Tolley looked at his hands.

"I. . .I. . .I," he began.

"All right, Brendan," Mojo interrupted, "Don't strain yourself."

"Jake?" He pushed the tabloid across to Jake's desk. "Filth or fun?"

"Well, I suppose I can see both sides," answered Jake, with a smile.

Mojo looked confused. "What's that supposed to mean?"

"It means he's a closet sexist," said Lindsey. "The worst kind."

Jake shrugged his shoulders. "You're entitled to your opinion," he replied. "I just think you're getting the whole thing out of proportion, that's all."

"Lin's not the only one who's got 'things' out of proportion," sniggered Dave Anderson, who was now standing behind Mojo admiring the photograph in question.

"Do you mind if we raise the tone of this discussion, please?" said Aftab. He turned towards Mojo. "Maurice, can't you see how demeaning a photo like that is for the model?"

"Yeah!" Lindsey took up Aftab's line of argument enthusiastically. "Absolutely. Turning herself into a sex object for the benefit of a slimy creeps like you," she pointed at Mojo, "just so she can earn a living."

"Nobody made her do it!" insisted Mojo.

"Made who do what?" Jake turned round and saw Charlie Cormack walk in the door. There was another girl behind her – freckle-faced, tanned and wearing a red down jacket.

"We were just talking about this," said Lindsey, holding up the relevant page of Mojo's newspaper.

"I see," said Charlie, taking off her Jaeger coat. "Well, she certainly has an incredible body."

"Thank you," said Mojo. "You see?" He turned to Aftab and Lindsey. "It's not just men who appreciate the artistic beauty of the female form."

"Hang on," said Charlie. "That's not what I meant." She laughed at the misunderstanding. "I meant incredible as in 'grotesque', not as in 'fantastic'. Still," she sat down and began taking books out of her bag, "if you're such an inadequate pervert that you need photos like that to— "

"I am *not* a pervert!" Mojo's voice was squeaky with defensiveness. "I'm an ordinary bloke."

"Same thing," muttered Lindsey Jordan.

"Good morning, everyone." Phil Hammond walked in, dumped his bag on one of the desks and began opening a window. A disconnected chorus of "Morning" went round the small, modern seminar room, then Lindsey asked: "How's your wife, sir?"

Mojo sulkily repeated the question in mime form for Jake's benefit, fluttering his eyelashes for added effect.

"No news," said Phil, turning round in a band of autumn sunlight, ". . . but thanks for asking. Now!" he rubbed his hands together and smiled, "I believe we have a new face in our midst." He took the register out of his bag and ran a finger down the list of names.

22

"Lauren. Is that right?" he asked, looking at the girl in the down jacket. "Lauren McGill?"

The girl nodded. "Right," she answered.

"Lauren's an exchange student from Redwood High School in San Rafael, California," explained Phil. "She'll be here with us at Portobello for the next twelve months." Jake looked across at the new girl. She was stocky (or maybe that was just the effect of the jacket), with wavy dark-brown hair and a square-jawed, open face. She seemed nervous.

"OK, down to business." Phil took up his customary teaching position, which meant sitting on rather than at his desk, with arms folded and legs swinging. "In the past couple of lessons we've talked about Media Studies in general." Several heads nodded. "All right. Today we're going to start work on the GCSE syllabus itself." He loosened his tie. "And what we'll be focussing on between now and Christmas is journalism. This stuff." He took the *Independent* out of his jacket pocket. "Oh, and that stuff, too," he added, pointing to the open copy of the *Sun* on Mojo's desk. Everyone laughed except Mojo, who tried to smile and didn't quite succeed.

"We'll be talking about magazines towards the end of term, but first I want to start with newspapers. Who produces them. What's in them. Who buys them. What effect they have. What's good and bad about them. The works."

Aftab Jehar put his hand up. "Sir, will we get a chance to visit a newspaper office? In Wapping, say?"

"That's up to you," answered Phil. "As I was saying last time, you'll have to do a project each term. Now if a group of you wanted to study how a local or perhaps even a national paper is run – fine! By all means."

"But we'd have to organize it all," said Aftab.

Phil nodded. "Yes – you and whoever else you're working with."

"Can we choose who we work with?" asked Lindsey.

"Same answer. It's up to you." Phil slid off his desk and began walking round the room as Dave and Lindsey both struck up conversations with their neighbours. "All right, all right. Settle down." He waited for silence. "You see, the point of the projects on this course is for you lot to do the work. I'll monitor how you're getting on, give you guidelines for presentation and deal with any problems that might crop up, but apart from that you're on your own."

"And how much time can we spend on each project?" asked Jake.

"Guess."

"It's up to us," said Jake, smiling. There was a chorus of low-key chuckles.

"In one." Phil had found his way to the front of the room again. "Look, I don't want to sound like a cracked record, but how long you spend on project work is a matter of how keen you are. We get six periods a week here in school, and you can do project work for half of that, but in your own time . . .?" He spread his hands.

"And what about the other three periods a week?" asked Charlie. "Is that all going to be textbook stuff?"

"Ahhh," said Phil. "What we in the teaching profession call 'textbook stuff'." He ran a hand round the back of his neck. "Some of it will be, but not all. For example, tomorrow afternoon I thought we might have a debate."

"Great!" said Dave Anderson. "I like a good argument."

"Do you mean a debate on newspapers and that?" asked Mojo.

"Yes," replied Phil. "Any ideas about what the motion might be?"

There was a moment's reflective silence, then Lindsey said, "I've got one. How about 'Are tabloids really newspapers?' " She glanced conspiratorially at Charlie.

24

"I'd be happy to propose it, and I think I know a few people who'd be prepared to *oppose* it, too."

"Sounds fine to me," said Phil. "All agreed?" There was a chorus of general approval. "Good." Phil leaned back against his desk. "Oh, and don't forget – I'll need to know your project titles by this time next week. Right – can I have some hush please?" He pulled a textbook out of his bag. "For the rest of this morning let's have a look at some of the major developments in British newspapers since 1980 . . ."

The next day at 10.45, Charlie, Aftab, Lindsey and Brendan emerged from Room 28 with an air of calm satisfaction on their faces. Behind them, Dave Anderson and Mojo seemed less pleased with the state of the world.

"How could you just *sit* there and say tabloids are comics for grown-ups!" spluttered Dave. "That's really patronising, that is."

"No, it's not," Charlie replied. "It's a fact!" She threw the last word over her shoulder without breaking her stride.

"Well, how come millions of people buy them every day?" taunted Mojo.

Charlie stopped suddenly so that Mojo nearly walked right into her. "Look," she said. "We've just been through all this. Basically most people get their news from the TV, right? Which leaves newspapers with one of two ways to go. Either they provide in-depth background or entertainment. Now if the tabloids want to provide gossip, bingo, innuendo and cheap titillation that's fine – it's a free country – I just don't think they should be allowed to call themselves newspapers, that's all. Anyway," she concluded with a demure smile, "you two are just angry because you lost the debate."

"That's got nothing to do with it!" Mojo squeakily protested. "It's class. That's what I'm talking about –

class. Your problem is you don't like the idea of popular papers for ordinary working people."

"Yeah – right," echoed Dave Anderson.

"Oh, grow up," snapped Lindsey. "Class is totally irrelevant to what we're talking about."

Aftab groaned. "Come on, you lot, we've only got ten minutes before the bell goes. I don't know about you but I need a cup of coffee." With that he pushed open a set of swing doors and led the group, still arguing, into the students' cafeteria.

From several yards down the corridor, Lauren McGill closed the door of her locker and gave a long, low whistle. "Is it always like this round here?"

Jake, who was jamming his baseball jacket into a neighbouring locker, replied with a chuckle. " 'Fraid so," he said. "Has been up to now, anyway."

"Here, let me help you," said Lauren and leaned her shoulder against Jake's locker until it closed.

"Thanks," he said, putting the key in his pocket. "For that you deserve a cup of coffee."

"OK, but on one condition."

"What's that?"

"We do *not* talk about the 'gutter' press."

Jake extended his right hand. "Agreed."

The students' cafeteria at Portobello College was hectic and noisy as usual. "Two coffees, please," Jake shouted above the din. Lauren, who was also standing at the counter, tapped him on the shoulder and pointed at the Media Studies group. They had taken over one corner of the room and were obviously still in the throes of a heated discussion.

"Shall we go over?" she asked. Jake turned round and shook his head.

"Too much arm-waving for my liking," he shouted. "Let's find somewhere quieter."

"So what do you make of Britain?" asked Jake once they'd installed themselves at a table by the window. "Is this your first time here?" Lauren smiled.

"Yep, and I think you could say I'm in total culture shock."

Jake smiled back. "I'm not surprised. How about the Cormacks? D'you get on all right with them?"

"Oh sure – they're terrific," said Lauren. "I mean, I knew them from when they lived in the States a couple of years back. And Charlie's great – she's really fun. No – I'm having a good time."

Jake examined her face. "But . . .?"

Lauren took a mouthful of coffee and allowed her bright, cheerful smile to fade a little. "Shows, huh? OK, well maybe I miss my family and friends a little – especially Kyle, that's my boyfriend." She looked out of the window at a line of beech trees which were already changing colour, then turned to Jake again. "But there you go. I guess everybody gets a few weeks of that when they first live in another country."

"Tell me about San Francisco," asked Jake. "I went to Vermont last year and helped at one of those summer camp things, but that's the nearest I've ever got."

"Bet you hated it," said Lauren with a grimace. "All those obnoxious spoilt brats running riot and you supposed to be in charge. Nightmare on wheels – am I right?"

Jake laughed. "You're not far wrong. Go on, though – tell me about San Francisco."

"OK," Lauren cleared her throat. "Let me see now. Well, San Francisco's kinda like a summer camp, too, only it's for spoilt adults." Jake laughed and she put a hand on his arm. "No. Wait. I'm joking. Let me start over." By now they were both laughing and didn't notice that Charlie had come up to their table.

"Time to go, Lauren," she said. "We've got French now."

Lauren looked at her watch. "Already?" She cast an apologetic glance across the table. "Guess we'll have to save this for another time."

"Yeah, OK." Jake stretched out his legs and put both hands behind his head, watching Charlie surreptitiously while the American girl got her books organized.

"Did you tell Jake about your Mom's invitation?" Lauren asked as the two of them were about to leave.

Charlie stopped. "Oh, no I didn't. It slipped my mind." She turned nonchalantly towards Jake, holding her jacket over one shoulder. "My mother wondered if you and *your* mother would like to come to lunch on Sunday."

Jake smiled. "Did she?" He coughed lightly against the back of his hand. "Well, I'll pass the message on to *my* mother. Meanwhile you can tell *your* mother that I'm sure we'd be delighted to accept and will confirm by telephone."

Lauren looked from one face to the other. "You guys – what's going on here?"

"I'll relay the message," said Charlie. Then, with Lauren still wearing a mystified expression, the two girls walked away. As they did so, Mojo came over and slipped quickly into Lauren's vacant chair.

"When are we going to have this band meeting, then?" he asked. "We haven't even got a name yet, you know."

Jake was following the retreating figures of Lauren and Charlie with his eyes. "Soon," he murmured vaguely.

Mojo smiled. "And you say *I've* got a one-track mind! You know something, I reckon you could be in there, my son."

Jake turned his head. "What?"

"With old Cormack. I overheard the bit about Sunday lunch." He wiggled his eyebrows in the manner which Jake had become totally familiar with over the six years of their friendship.

"Well, you're wrong," he replied. "In the first place Mrs

28

Cormack knows my mum and that's why she's invited us. In the second place 'old Cormack' thinks I'm a prat, which is exactly what I feel about her, too, after that business I told you about at the parents 'do' and her performance just now in Media Studies. And in the *third* place . . ." Mojo was still relentlessly wiggling his eyebrows. "Mo!" Jake insisted. "I – do – not – fancy – her. All right? Got it?!"

"Yeah, right," grinned Mojo. "And the Pope's not Catholic." He stood up. "Come on, we're going to be late for Music."

Two days later, Jake and Mojo finally had their band meeting in the college's soundproof rehearsal room.

"OK," said Jake. "I've got a list of names here. Well – four – but they're all great. Serious contenders. Ready?"

Mojo closed his eyes. "Ready."

"Skyline."

"No."

"W11."

"What?"

"W11. West eleven. It's where we live, moron."

"No."

"The Barry Manilow Fan Club."

Mojo opened one eye and gave Jake half a hard stare. "Moving – right – along," he said through clenched teeth.

"Nexus."

There was a short pause. "Say that one again."

"Nexus."

"What's it mean?"

"It means – well, it's like a focal point or a group of things that stick together. At least I think that's what it means. It's Latin."

Mojo sniffed pensively and looked at the thick white

ceiling tiles over his head. "Not bad. Nexus. Yeah – that's good. What do *you* think?"

Jake perused his list. "Well, the one I was really rooting for was 'The Barry Manilow Fan Club' – but since that got the big E . . . yeah, all right. 'Nexus' it is." He paused. "You don't think it sounds too . . . you know . . . too pretentious?"

Mojo began plucking a bass riff while he thought this over. "Nah." Then, a few notes later, he said, "I'm going round to see Carlton tonight. Wanna come? He says he's got some great new imports – jazz funk stuff."

Jake shook his head. "Can't. There's some bloke coming over for dinner and I'm supposed to be there."

"Who is he then, this bloke?"

"Oh, just someone Mum's been seeing for a while," said Jake casually.

Mojo stopped playing. "What? Like a boyfriend?"

"Yeah – I suppose."

"Have you met him?"

Jake cleared his throat. "No. That's what tonight's in aid of." He picked out three random notes on the piano. "Anyway, I can't go round to Carlton's."

"Right."

"Right."

Mojo began playing again and once he'd picked up the tempo Jake came in with some jazz chords on the piano. The two of them improvised for a few minutes, then suddenly Jake's hands froze on the keys. "I've just thought of something," he said. "What are we going to do for Hammond's journalism project? We're supposed to let him know by this afternoon. I'd completely forgotten about it." Mojo, who was experimenting with some tricky harmonics, smiled but didn't respond. "Hello, Earth to Johnson, Earth to Johnson," said Jake through cupped hands – "Do you read me, over?"

Mojo stopped playing.

"I said, what are we going to do for this journalism project? We've got to decide – now!"

Mojo sighed and put down his bass. "Relax," he said. "You worry too much, that's your trouble. Uncle Maurice has got it all sussed out."

Jake changed position on the piano stool uneasily. "Has he?"

Mojo grinned, then linked his fingers, cracked them and leaned forwards.

" 'Course he has. Now then," he began, "let's review what everybody else is doing. Aftab and Brendan are putting together this '*Millenium*' thing, right? – all the stories they reckon are going to be in the papers on January 1st, 2000."

"Right."

"And Dave and Lauren are writing a 'Day in the Life' blurb about Wapping and new technology and all that."

"Right again."

"Which leaves . . ." here Mojo paused for dramatic effect, ". . . Lindsey and old Cormack." Jake stared at him blankly.

"And what's their project going to be?" Mojo pressed.

"A local paper. Mo, what's all this about?"

"What kind of local paper?"

"A 'good news' local paper."

"Why?"

Jake sighed, but knew he'd get nowhere unless he played along. "Because they're fed up with papers that only print scandal and gossip and focus on bad news," he recited like a six-year-old saying his tables. "They want to prove it's possible to produce one with — " he did the inverted commas with his fingers " ' — a totally positive approach'."

The beginnings of a Machiavellian smile had now started to play round the edges of Mojo's mouth. "Which is where my idea comes in," he said. "Can't you guess what it is?"

31

There was a short pause, then gradually, very gradually, the same smile appeared on Jake's face, too. "You want to set up a paper in competition with theirs."

Mojo formed an 'O' with the thumb and forefinger of his right hand.

"You want to get your own back on them for all that Page Three business and the debate."

"Give the man a cigar," said Mojo. "But!" he leaned even further forward, "the beauty of the whole thing is that theirs will be feeble and ours will be MEGA! We'll put in all the stuff people *really* want to read about – *they'll* just be doing guff about bob-a-job week and whist drives at the over-60s club. Net result: they get panned and we win all the laurels. Waddya reckon?"

Jake grinned and pulled the lobe of his right ear thoughtfully. "Hmmmm."

"Imagine Lindsey's face when she finds out."

Jake's grin broadened. "And old Cormack's."

Mojo doubled up as his feet performed an impromptu drumroll of ecstatic anticipation on the wooden floor. Then he suddenly straightened again, exhaled happily and held out both palms. "So. Are we on?"

"Yep!" Jake slapped the palms and offered his own for the second half of the ritual. "We're on."

Chapter 3

Kay Shepherd took a deep breath of night air and leaned contentedly against the front door. She was wearing what she called her "upmarket peasant" dress and watching a blue Escort parked across the street. After a moment it slowly began to pull away and Kay waved. A hand emerged from the side window and waved back, then the car drove off and she went inside again. In the dining room Jake was prodding aimlessly at a piece of Camembert on the plate in front of him. He heard the front door close and looked up as his mother walked in. "Dishes?" he asked unenthusiastically. Kay screwed up her nose, sat down and lit a thin cheroot.

"In a minute," she said, removing a sliver of tobacco from the tip of her tongue. The room was silent for a moment apart from a muted Vivaldi concerto in the background, then Kay began examining the nails of her right hand. "So what did you think of him?" she asked casually. Jake resumed prodding the piece of Camembert.

"Graham? He was all right."

"All right?" Her voice was discreetly questioning.

"Yeah – seemed like a nice bloke."

Kay nodded slowly.

"Bit nervous though," Jake went on.

"That was because of you."

"Me?!"

"Hmmm." Kay smiled and tipped her ash onto a side plate. "All those questions you kept asking."

Jake shrugged his shoulders. "I like to find out about people. Nothing wrong with that." He laid down the knife he'd been holding and leaned his forearms on the table. "You didn't tell me he was in the police."

"Didn't I?"

"No."

Kay frowned slightly. "Does it matter?"

"No, I suppose not," answered Jake, retreating back into his chair. "Seems funny, though, doesn't it – a copper getting nervous 'cos somebody my age asks him a few questions." He gave a short, hollow laugh. "Makes a change, mind you. Usually it's the other way round."

Kay stubbed out her cheroot, leaned across the table and took her son's hand. "Jake."

"What?"

"If you didn't like him, just say so. I won't be angry or anything."

Jake kept his eyes on the table. "It's not that. I didn't 'not like' him. It's just . . ."

"What?"

"Well . . . why did you put Dad's photo away tonight? The one on the mantelpiece? It's not there, is it?"

After a brief pause Kay gradually withdrew her hand. "Oh Jake," she said softly. "I didn't move it because of Graham. Is that what you thought?"

"Why then?"

Kay sighed. "I just put it in my room when I was clearing up this afternoon. I wanted to have flowers on the mantelpiece and there wasn't enough space. That's all, OK?" There was no reply. "OK?"

"OK."

Eight bars of Vivaldi's baroque harmonies drifted round the candlelit room with no interruption. Finally, Jake pushed back his chair and stood up. "I've got some reading to do for English tomorrow," he said. "Is it all right if I go up to my room now? I mean, we can do the dishes first if you like."

Kay looked at him and shook her head. "No, that's OK, love. You go up. I'll do them."

"You sure?"

"Yeah."

"Right," said Jake. He remained standing for a moment, then walked towards the door, where he seemed to make a decision. Turning he said, "Look, I dunno what I'm on about. Don't pay any attention. I suppose I'm still a bit – you know – Dad and all that." He paused. "Graham *is* a nice bloke and I *did* like him." Mother and son looked at each other across the room. "Great meal by the way," said Jake, scratching his chin.

"Thanks."

"See you in the morning, then."

Kay smiled. "Goodnight." She watched the door close and listened as Jake went upstairs. Then, exhaling with a tiny shudder, she stood up and carried three coffee mugs into the kitchen.

"They're here!" said Lauren from the bay window in Charlie's bedroom. Down below a pink 2CV was crunching up the Cormacks' elegantly maintained gravel drive. Having got no reaction the first time, Lauren repeated her news, this time looking over one shoulder. "I said the Shepherds are here."

"Really?" replied Charlie with studied indifference. She was lying face down on the embroidered counterpane of her bed, flicking through the pages of French *Vogue*.

Lauren sighed. "Charlie, what is it with you today? You've been behaving like Miss Piggy with pre-menstrual tension all morning." More flicking of pages.

"What do you think it is?" came a voice from the bed. Then, shutting *Vogue* decisively, Charlie turned over and sat up. "Infantile creeps," she muttered, more or less to herself.

Lauren adopted a half-lotus position on the window seat and folded her arms. "Ahhh – I think I get it now. This is about Jake and Mojo, right?"

Charlie breathed out hard through her nose, then broke into an unflattering imitation of Jake's north London accent. " 'Well Phil, since Charlie and Lindsey are so confident their paper's going to be a success, we thought they wouldn't mind a bit of healthy competition.' Healthy! Hah!"

Lauren suppressed a smile. "OK, so it wasn't the most mature choice of project in the world, but look on the bright side. This way you and Lindsey get the chance to *prove* you're right. Don't get mad, Charlie – that's what they want. Just make sure your paper's better than theirs."

Charlie got up and moved to the dressing table. On it there was a blue folder which she picked up, permitting herself a smile as she did so. "Oh, don't worry on that score," she said. "Lindsey and I had a *long* talk last night and came up with a few ideas. We'll come out on top all right." She began plaiting her hair energetically. "It's just their sheer male bloody-mindedness I object to."

The front door bell rang.

"Charlotte! Lauren!" called Gudrun Cormack's voice from downstairs. "Could one of you answer that, please? I'm having a crisis with the hollandaise." Up in Charlie's room the atmosphere lightened as both girls spontaneously grinned, then Lauren ran onto the landing and called down, "It's OK – I'll go." At the top of the stairs she looked back into Charlie's room. "I know you're angry," she said, "but don't declare war just yet, OK? And try not to snipe at Jake for the next few hours. Remember – this is supposed to be a friendly social event."

Charlie gazed at her in theatrical amazement. "Snipe? Me!" She smiled demurely. "Heaven forbid."

"Promise?"

This time the smile was genuine. "I promise. Now why don't you let them in? I'll be down in a minute."

Before lunch Gudrun insisted on showing Kay round the garden, which featured several exotic specimens including a pair of Chinese willow trees. Meanwhile Lauren led Jake into the kitchen where he took stock of his impressive surroundings while she poured two glasses of white wine and began laying the table. They chatted amiably for a few minutes, then Charlie appeared. "Oh, hello Jake," she said, walking briskly into the room. "How are you?"

"Fine. You too?"

"Hmm, yes. I'm terribly well."

"Good. Good."

Lauren followed this exchange attentively as if she was watching a tennis match, then at the first pause broke in with, "Charlie – your Mom said would you mind making the salad while she's showing Mrs Shepherd round the garden. All the stuff's in the fridge."

"Right," said Charlie, picking up a knife and smiling at Jake. "Better get started then, hadn't I?"

Conversation stopped for a few moments while the girls got on with what they were doing and Jake looked round the room. Then he asked, "So where's your old man, Charlie?"

"My father's in Milan," came the reply. "He was supposed to be coming back this morning, but apparently his flight's been delayed. I expect he'll turn up at some stage, though."

"What's he doing in Milan?"

"Oh, business," Charlie replied noncommittally. She was slicing tomatoes on a massive butcher's block table with precision and vigour.

Jake watched her and smiled. "Ahhh – business." He took a sip of wine. "What is it he does exactly? I thought he worked in the City." Charlie had now moved to the sink and was washing a bunch of spring onions.

"He does, but he travels a lot, too. He's an investment broker." She half turned. "I presume you know what a broker does?" Lauren looked up from the napkin she was folding and shot a warning glance across the kitchen.

"Yeah – sort of," answered Jake, whose understanding of what brokers did was, to put it mildly, thin.

Charlie rubbed her nose with the back of a wet hand and decided not to pursue the topic. Instead she asked, "What about *your* father? What does he do?"

There was a short silence. "My dad's not around any more."

"Ah – does that mean he and your mother are divorced?"

"No." Jake looked up from his wine glass. "It means he's dead. He died of cancer last year."

Charlie turned round, a flush of shock and embarrassment rising in her face. "Oh God, I'm sorry," she said. "I didn't know. I assumed . . ."

"That's all right," interrupted Jake. "Don't worry about it."

"But I . . ."

"Charlie," his voice was firm. "It's OK. Really." The room suddenly became very quiet. "Anyway . . ." Jake put on a slightly lame smile and turned to Lauren. "Since we're talking about fathers . . . what's yours? – movie-producer? Oil tycoon? Hot-shot lawyer? Got to be something high-powered if he's a Californian."

"Uh-uh," replied Lauren, echoing Jake's smile to help him over the awkward moment. "Wrong on all counts. My Mom's the hot-shot – she runs a chain of boutiques. As for Dad – well, he was born in Idaho and he's a second-hand-car dealer. Not what you'd call glamorous, I'm afraid."

In itself this wasn't a particularly funny remark, but for their different reasons Charlie, Jake and Lauren were all glad of the opportunity to laugh. Somehow after that the whole situation felt much more relaxed and conversation began to flow quite naturally. Jake got the two girls to describe how they first met in America and in return he told them lengthy anecdotes about a disastrous Greyhound bus trip he'd made the previous summer between Vermont and Washington. By the time he reached the end of his account the table was set and Charlie's salad was complete. She poured them all another glass of wine and looked out of the kitchen window with a sigh.

"Mother's in absolutely full flow. I can tell by the way she's flinging her arms around. Look – she'll be ages yet. Why don't we go into the sitting room and listen to some music? Everything's ready in here now."

The Cormacks' sitting room was roughly as big as a tennis court. It featured three ivory-coloured sofas, an open fireplace, several abstract paintings and a vast smoked-glass coffee table loaded with thick, glossy magazines, all of which Jake completely ignored because as soon as he walked in he saw the grand piano.

"Gordon Bennett, you've got a Steinway," he breathed, reverentially moving towards the piano like a lovestruck sleepwalker. Lowering himself onto the padded stool he suddenly remembered where he was and looked across at Charlie. "Is it OK if . . .?"

"Go right ahead," she replied, flopping onto one of the sofas. "I think you'll find some Chopin preludes there and a few Mozart pieces."

"Oh, right," murmured Jake. He riffled through the copies of sheet music, selected one and placed it carefully on the stand in front of him. "Ready?" he enquired, glancing across to the sofa where Charlie and Lauren had both arranged themselves in languid postures.

"This is soooo Jane Austen," said Lauren. Jake coughed delicately, flicked a pair of imaginary tails away from the piano stool and addressed himself to the keys. Taking a deep breath he raised his eyes to the ceiling and held the pose for a moment. Then, having achieved total inspiration he suddenly crouched down over the keyboard and broke into a spirited boogie-woogie rendition of "Yes Sir, That's My Baby."

"He's really *good*," Lauren whispered to Charlie once

they'd both stopped laughing. Charlie raised an amused eyebrow and took in the figure at the Steinway, all pumping feet and splayed hands.

"Hmmm," she replied casually. "I suppose so." She paused. "If you like that sort of thing."

One of the topics of conversation towards the end of lunch was Kay's first one-woman exhibition which had recently been commissioned by a small gallery in Camden Town.

"How exciting!" said Gudrun, widening her eyes. "You must be thrilled. It's just what we dreamed of all those years ago. When is it?" From across the table Jake found himself staring at Gudrun Cormack. Never in his whole life had he seen anybody so seriously in "hostess" mode. Every gesture and facial expression was perfectly presented as if she was on stage. Yes, that was it – that's what made him feel so uneasy – the whole thing felt like a slightly manic performance.

"April," replied Kay, turning an art-deco coffee cup in her hands. "But actually I haven't had any time to be thrilled. I mean, I am of course, but there's so much to do. I'll have to work flat out between now and Christmas if I'm going to get everything ready. Including . . ." she indicated Jake across the table, "a portrait of his Lordship here."

Charlie had a spoonful of peach melba halfway to her mouth. She lowered it.

"You're doing a portrait of Jake, Mrs Shepherd?"

"Yes," replied Kay. "It's nearly ready in fact."

"How very interesting," said Charlie thoughtfully. She turned to Lauren. "You know," she remarked, "that's just the sort of thing Lindsey and I could do a feature on for the arts section of our newspaper. We could have a photo of it and everything. It would be terribly good publicity for Mrs Shepherd's exhibition, too, wouldn't it?"

"What a wonderful idea!" said Gudrun brightly. She beamed at Kay. "Don't you agree?"

"Uh-yes," said Kay, simultaneously noticing the expression of unsuppressed horror on Jake's face, but by then it was too late to turn back.

"Oh good!" exclaimed Charlie, grinning mischievously. "That's settled then." She paused. "Unless Jake has any objections, of course?"

Jake had plenty of objections and was just about to raise them when the door behind him suddenly opened and Antony Cormack walked in. "Darling, there you are!" exclaimed Gudrun. "We were beginning to get worried. Oh you poor thing, you look exhausted."

Antony smiled wanly as he pulled up a chair next to his wife and pecked her on the cheek. She was right, thought Jake, he did look tired. What was it Cora Peters called the bags under her eyes? Oh yes, "sub-ocular luggage". Well, Charlie's dad was sporting a couple of hefty facial suitcases.

"Hello, folks," he said, pouring himself a large drink and winking at Charlie. "Hello, C – how's tricks?"

She smiled. "I'm fine. Dad, you remember the Shepherds? They were at the Portobello parents' evening a few weeks ago."

Antony looked at Kay and Jake. "Ah yes," he said, clearly not recognizing them at all. "Of course, of course. Nice to see you again."

Twenty minutes later Jake discreetly excused himself in the middle of a lengthy monologue on the Milan Stock Exchange and went in search of the loo. On his way back he met Lauren coming up the stairs. They stopped and gave each other an understanding smile. "I needed a breather, too," she remarked and Jake chuckled. After that neither of them seemed to know quite what came next, then Jake had an idea.

"I was talking to Aftab the other day," he began, "and he said you play the sax. Is that right?"

Lauren nodded enthusiastically. "Yeah – tenor. It's in

41

my room. Wanna see it?" She paused. "Although maybe we should . . ."

Jake grinned. "Nah – they won't miss us for a few minutes. Come on."

Lauren's attic room, which could only be reached by climbing a stepladder, was triangular, sky-blue and spectacularly untidy. "Wow!" said Jake, stepping over a scattered assortment of clothes and books on his way to the window. "Great view!" Below him the green expanse of Holland Park dotted with Sunday strollers stretched into the distance. Leaning on the window sill Jake began watching a group of kids knocking a Subbuteo-sized football around, then the sudden, breathy vibrato of a tenor saxophone made him turn and smile. Lauren was leaning against the wall, eyebrows raised, cheeks rounded, playing an old Glen Miller tune – "String of Pearls". She was good. Jake waited until the tune was over, then applauded warmly. "That was terrific! Really terrific! How long have you been playing?" Lauren screwed up her eyes.

"Four years? No, five. I started taking lessons in ninth grade."

"And do you play other stuff, too – apart from jazz, I mean?"

"Oh sure – rock, funk, hip-hop . . ." she started to laugh, ". . . basically anything except country and western."

Jake watched thoughtfully as she put the saxophone back in its case. "Listen", he began. "You wouldn't be interested in joining a band, would you?"

"A band? What kind of band?"

Jake grinned. "Well, me and Mojo basically. We've been writing songs and stuff for a couple of years, but now we've decided to get more serious. Mojo's got this mate, you see – Carlton – and Carlton reckons he can get us some gigs. Pubs – that sort of thing. We've even got a name."

"Oh yeah?"

"Nexus."

Lauren clicked shut the saxophone case. "Nexus," she repeated softly. "So do you play mostly jazz or what?"

"Bit like you," replied Jake. "Jazz, rock, funk – whatever takes our fancy, really. More jazz funk than anything else though." He hoisted himself up onto the window sill as somewhere downstairs a telephone began to ring.

"Why don't you bring your sax along to the music room on Tuesday? We're having a rehearsal after school and you can find out for yourself what sort of stuff we play." He opened his hands. "What've you got to lose?"

"Nothing, I guess." Lauren smiled happily, but then a cloud of doubt suddenly scudded across her face. "Except . . ."

"Except what?" Jake searched her face before one corner of his mouth turned up ruefully. "Oh, I get it. Except Charlie might not approve."

Lauren looked embarrassed. "Yeah." Neither of them spoke for a moment. Then, as if to break the silence, Antony Cormack's voice called from downstairs.

"Lauren! Telephone!"

"OK!" she called back, and was part-way down the stepladder before she stopped and looked across at Jake. He was morosely making small figures of eight in mid-air with one tennis shoe. "Look," she said. "This is crazy. If you and Charlie are having some kind of dumb feud over the Media Studies journalism thing, that's your affair. Why should I let it affect me?" She smiled. "I'd love to come on Tuesday."

"Really?"

"Really. We'll talk about it at school tomorrow, OK?" Then she was gone.

Left alone, Jake thought over the possibility of Nexus becoming a three-piece band and watched the footballers in Holland Park for a minute before following Lauren downstairs. He'd only got as far as the landing when he came to an abrupt halt. Visible through the half-open door on his left was a blue folder with the words "Portobello Gazette" on the cover. It was lying next to a chair and partially hidden by the blue angora scarf which Charlie regularly wore to school. It *must* be her room. It could only be her room. For a long moment Jake stood motionless while a variety of conflicting possibilities went through his mind. Finally, casting a furtive glance down the stairwell to make sure the coast was clear, he slipped through the door, closing it behind him. "Just a quick look," he told himself, surreptitiously opening the folder. Inside there were several neatly-typewritten pages of notes, the first of which was headed STATEMENT OF INTENT. Aware that his heart was beating much faster than usual, Jake began to read it.

"The aim of the *Portobello Gazette* will be to present a positive, unbiased, constructive view of local community news aimed at the youth market. Why? Because in recent years most of the newspapers bought by teenagers – namely the tabloids – have sunk from the gutter to the sewer in search of scandal and sensationalism." Jake permitted himself a barely audible chuckle before reading on. "Through the *Portobello Gazette* we want to show that all news need not be bad news catering to a Page-Three mentality eager to have its own prejudices massaged by . . ."

"OK, OK," chortled Jake. "We get the drift." He flicked over to the next page, read it quickly and felt the smile leave his face. The following two pages seemed to depress him even more, and then he came to one headed "CONTENTS LIST". Scanning the items on the list Jake became totally engrossed as he tried to memorize as many as possible – so engrossed that for a moment he didn't react when the door opened. It was only as Charlie's voice exclaimed, "What the . . .!" that he whirled guiltily round. She was standing in the doorway, motionless and perfectly framed like an illustration in a 1920's detective novel. "How dare you! Of all the . . .!" Complete sentences seemed beyond her power. As if recognizing this she gave up trying to produce any and resorted to action instead, striding towards Jake, wrenching the folder from his hands and clasping it protectively to her body.

"So what happened then?" asked Mojo, his mouth hanging open with disbelief. "What do you think?" replied Jake miserably. It was three hours since Charlie had discovered him reading the blue folder and now he was at Mojo's house, sitting on a beaten-up wicker chair in the Johnson's back garden. Dusk was falling. "First she gave me a mouthful about being in her room – then she went on about what an immature rat I was, exactly the type who *would* go snooping around, and how if you and me wanted to set up a rival paper that was just fine and dandy with her and Lindsey 'cos they'd wipe the floor with us. There was more, but . . ." he trailed off and stared disconsolately at a rhododendron bush through the gathering gloom. Somewhere in the distance a dog was barking.

"And you just stood there?"

"What else could I do? Talk about having me by the short and curlies. Then of course we had to go back downstairs and be all nice and polite for another hour before Mum and I could get out. That was the worst part. Oh Mo, it was horrible" – he buried his face in his hands – "horrible."

Mojo nodded sympathetically. "So what was on the contents list?"

Jake heaved a sigh and changed position with a crackle of wicker against baseball jacket. "Well," he began, looking up. "You know we reckoned it was all going to be stories about battling grannies and tips on flower-arranging . . .?"

Mojo leaned forwards. "Isn't it?"

Jake shook his head despondently. "There's a piece on Portobello kids who've recently got jobs – interviews and everything – a big feature on racial integration, some stuff on that new sports centre that's just opened – a thing about drug rehabilitation, an arts section – what else? – oh, I forget, but it was a very long list. 'Course they'll probably change it all after today, but the point is they're miles ahead of us, Mo. We've got to get our act together and soon, otherwise we won't stand a chance."

Mojo slapped his knees, got up and began stalking round the seated figure of Jake and his own deserted wicker chair. "OK, OK – positive thinking – that's what we need here," he intoned. "First, let's go over the basics. Hammond says both papers have to be four pages long, right?"

"Right."

"And they've both got to be ready by December 4th."

"Also right."

"And so far all we've got for the *Portobello Post* is a few ideas on the back of an envelope." Jake nodded soberly. "OK." Mojo stopped pacing. "Sounds to me like we need an emergency editorial meeting."

"When?"

"Now."

"Where?"

"My room."

Jake stood up. "Let's go."

Mojo's room was a shrine to modern music. Every inch of available space was covered with posters and photos, while his record collection ran the entire length of one wall. Opposite that was the sound system, the bed and a giant red bean bag. At half past ten Jake put down the pen and pad he was holding and slumped back against this last item. "I'm knackered," he said.

"Never mind that," murmured Mojo, not even looking down from his position on the bed. "Let's go through the check-list again. I want to make sure we haven't forgotten anything."

Jake opened his eyes with difficulty and focussed them on Mojo's eager face bent over the piece of paper in his hands. "Mo," he said as calmly as possible, "We've just done that. Schedules – typesetting – what's going in the first issue – where the photos are coming from – it's all here," he waved his pad in the air.

Mojo wasn't satisfied. "So who's doing the truancy story – you or me?"

"You." Jake yawned hugely and consulted his notes. "You're also doing the gossip column, the vox pop, the horoscopes, and you're talking to this girl Carlton knows about the possibility of a Page 3 photo." He lowered the pad. "Are you *sure* that's a good idea?"

Mojo's eyebrows embarked on one of their regular jiggling bouts. "Her name's Desirée. Just wait till you see her – she'll knock you out."

"So will old Cormack," muttered Jake, wincing. "Listen – this Desirée, she *is* over sixteen, isn't she?"

"Yeah, yeah, yeah. She's a go-go dancer in a club in Harlesden."

"Oh, very tasteful," replied Jake, returning to his pad. He sighed. "And while you're doing that lot, I'm in charge of design, layout, the record and gig reviews . . ."

"I thought *I* was doing that!"

"Well, tough, you're not . . . the soap up-dates, the strip cartoon and the article on drugs at Portobello." He looked up. "Now will you please relax. We've done everything we can for tonight. Besides, it's late and I want to get home."

Mojo knuckle-rubbed his eyes. "Yeah, all right."

"Oh, I nearly forgot to tell you," said Jake, putting on his jacket. "I've invited Lauren to the rehearsal on Tuesday."

"Lauren?"

"Yeah. You know Aftab said she had a sax? Well, I heard her play this afternoon and she's good – really excellent, in fact. You don't mind if she comes along for a bit of a jam session, do you?"

"Fine by me," said Mojo. "The more the merrier." He stretched luxuriously as Jake walked to the door, then raised one finger aloft. "There's something I forgot to tell *you*, too. Guess what?"

Jake turned. "What?"

"I've got a job! Well, sort of. From now on, every Wednesday and Saturday night I'll be spinning some totally crucial platters at the Jamboree Bag."

"That club where Carlton works? You're going to be a DJ there?"

"Yeah – good wheeze, eh? They needed somebody part-time for a few months and Carlton suggested me. First night's next Wednesday."

Jake grinned. "Great."

"I'm pretty impressed myself," said Mojo. "Anyway, I'll tell you all about it at school tomorrow. Now clear off, eh – I reckon it's time we both got some beauty sleep."

Walking home from Mojo's house, Jake tried to piece together some of the recent events in his life. Portobello, Nexus, Graham whatsisname, the paper, Charlie Cormack . . . There was a lot to think about and most of it made him feel vaguely uneasy. Of course it might all turn out for the best, but then again . . .

Passing underneath the neon hum of streetlights he sidestepped a puddle and started down Antrobus Road – his road. It was deserted except for two lines of parked cars – perfect conditions, Jake noticed, for re-adjusting a few wing mirrors like he and Mojo used to do when they were kids. He smiled at the memory, carried on walking and was nearly home when he drew level with a silver

48

BMW similar to the Cormacks'. At that point tempta-
tion overwhelmed him and Jake gave its wing mirror a
good, sharp nudge for old times' sake that left it pointing skywards. "Take that," he muttered, breaking into a
throaty chuckle. Then, whistling and feeling altogether
more cheerful, he strolled up the moonlit path of No.
64 and let himself in.

Chapter 4

At 2.30 on Tuesday afternoon Cora Peters marched into Room 28, raised both hands and shouted "Quiet please!" Then, once the noise level had dropped, she made an announcement. "Mr Hammond's been called to the phone and he's going to be a few minutes late. In the interim I'm sure you can all find something constructive to do." She smiled knowingly. "Especially those of you in my English set who haven't handed in your essays on *Troilus and Cressida*. I mention no names, but follow my eyes." Here she looked pointedly at Mojo who immediately developed an intense interest in the stickers on his pencil case.

"Witch," he muttered, as she swept out of the room.

"So anyway . . ." Lindsey resumed the conversation she'd been having with Brendan ". . . *Millenium*'s definitely going to be ready by next week, is it?"

"Oh yes," beamed Brendan. "In fact it's practically finished already. I've still got a short piece on the morality of in-vitro genetic engineering to write, and Aftab wants to re-draft his article on the creation of a Palestinian homeland, don't you, Aftab? – apart from that, though . . ."

"Yes, apart from that we're ready," echoed Aftab.

"But of course we haven't done any actual reporting like you have," he added with an apologetic smile to Lindsey. "*Millenium*'s more of a pure academic project, isn't it, Bren?"

"Mmmm," Brendan nodded vigorously. "Which is why it's longer."

"How many pages did you end up doing?" asked Dave Anderson.

"Sixteen," replied Aftab. "But they're not really pages in the traditional sense – we've put it all on a word-processor disc, you see. "That's what we'll be handing in."

Lindsey made an impressed face. "Very futuristic."

"Hardly," said Dave. "That's what most papers do already – it's just direct input journalism. Here, have a look at these." He pulled some 8″ x 10″ photos out of his briefcase and lobbed them onto Lindsey's desk. They showed the very latest in newspaper offices.

"Oh great – the prints came through!" exclaimed Lauren, who'd just walked in with Charlie.

"Yeah – got them back this morning," said Dave. "They've come out really well, too."

"Are these the shots you took at Wapping last week?" asked Charlie, looking over Lindsey's shoulder. Lauren hung her down jacket over a chair and did likewise.

"Yeah. We had such a good time that day, didn't we, Dave?"

"I'll say," agreed Dave. "That bloke Phil knows on *The Times* is amazing – took us round everything."

"Certainly did," agreed Lauren, absorbed in looking at the glossy prints. After a few seconds she straightened up, apparently satisfied with their quality. "Boy, I wouldn't want to work there, though," she added.

"Why not?" asked Lindsey. "Looks wonderful. Clean, modern, quiet – must be paradise compared to how newspaper offices were twenty years ago."

"Yeah," Lauren allowed reluctantly. "But there was something about it – I don't know – something . . ."

"Soul-less?" suggested Charlie.

"Right – 'soul-less'," Lauren took up the adjective eagerly. "All those people just sitting around tapping on keyboards and staring at VDUs hour after hour. There was no 'oomph' – no 'hold the front page' – no green eyeshades – you know what I mean?"

"Well, there's going to be plenty of 'oomph' in the

Portobello Gazette, I can promise you that," said Lindsey, with a smirk in Jake and Mojo's general direction.

"Yes, how's the *Gazette* coming along?" asked Brendan, polishing his glasses on a large white handkerchief. "I must say you've been very quiet about it these past few weeks."

"Quiet but confident I think you'd call us," asserted Charlie, flicking her hair back with a swift gesture.

"Absolutely," Lindsey concurred, folding her arms. "We'll be ready on December 4th, you needn't worry about that. Whether our so-called 'competitors' can say the same I don't know, but I'd imagine it's highly unlikely."

Aftab gave a long low whistle. "Tough talk!" He leaned his chair back and looked over one shoulder to where Jake and Mojo were sitting. "Would either of you two gentlemen care to comment on behalf of the *Portobello Post*?"

"Not really," said Jake amiably, looking up from some homework he'd been catching up on. "Why don't we all just wait and see what happens?"

"Yes, well, I don't think that's very difficult to predict," countered Lindsey smugly.

"Meaning?" enquired Mojo.

"Meaning the *Gazette*'s unbiased, positive approach will put your tawdry little rag well and truly in the shade." Lindsey completed her statement by blowing a kiss at Mojo, who returned the compliment with sarcastic knobs on to an accompaniment of sarcastic whoops and wails from various parts of the room.

"Oh right," Jake nodded understandingly. "And this is an example of your unbiased, positive approach, is it? – slagging off the opposition before you've even seen it."

"I think Jake might have a point there, don't you?" suggested Brendan tentatively.

Charlie ignored Brendan's remark completely and fixed Jake with a steely glare. "I wouldn't get too high and mighty if I were you," she muttered darkly. "Not after what I caught you doing last weekend." There was a short, highly-charged pause.

"What's all this then?" grinned Dave Anderson eagerly. "What happened last weekend?"

Charlie didn't break eye contact with Jake. "Do you want to tell the story, or shall I?" she enquired. At this point Lauren groaned and Mojo whispered "Oops!", but Dave, Aftab, Brendan and Lindsey all looked expectantly at Jake.

"Can't stop!"

Everyone turned round. Phil Hammond was standing in the doorway looking breathless, dishevelled and not altogether rational. He was carrying a crash helmet. "The hospital just phoned," he explained, staring wildly round at the amazed faces in front of him. "It's the baby . . . I've got to . . . you know . . ." he waved one hand in the direction of the staff car park. "Just get on with something from the textbook, OK?" Then he was gone.

After school, Jake, Lauren and Mojo met in the music studio as arranged.

"OK – this next one's called 'What's Up?' " said Jake about forty-five minutes into the rehearsal. He rubbed both palms down the sides of his jeans. "Ready Mo?" Mojo nodded. "Here we go then. A-one, a-two, a-one, two, three, four."

The opening chords of an up-tempo blues, chunky, powerful and rhythmic, spilled out across the room to where Lauren was sitting on a high stool. She listened for a few seconds, then began to weave a saxophone solo around the bass and piano lines, feeling her way at first with short runs. This went on for several bars, gradually building and growing more confident until, like someone jumping off a diving board, Lauren moved into a completely different gear. Stepping down off the stool with

53

her sax clamped to one side, knees bent and head back, she broke into a stream of high, wailing arpeggios. The last one ended in a completely pure top C during which Mojo glanced across to the piano and raised his eyebrows in stunned astonishment. Jake nodded and grinned.

Just then the door opened. It was Angela Mogridge, Tom Busby's secretary. Statuesque and efficient-looking in an immaculate grey twinset she stood in the open doorway smiling and holding her spectacles. "Sorry to disturb you," she began sympathetically as "What's Up?" broke off into an abrupt silence, "but it's five past five and I've got to lock up now."

Mojo checked his watch. "Blimey! It is and all. Sorry, Mrs M, we completely lost track of the time."

Angela Mogridge held up a "That's OK" hand. "Actually, I've been outside listening for the last few minutes," she confessed. "You're very good, you know – and Lauren, I didn't know you could play the saxophone! Does this mean you're a member of Jake and Maurice's group now?"

Jake folded his arms. "She is if she wants to be – right, Mo?"

"You bet," Mojo agreed. Cradling his bass he looked at Lauren. "What do you say?"

Lauren's eyes sparkled. "Are you guys serious?" They both nodded. "OK, then," she laughed. "The answer's 'yes'."

Twenty minutes later Lauren and Mojo came out of High Street Kensington tube station in the middle of the rush hour. Above them a spectacular mackerel-patterned sunset was just beginning to fade. "So anyway," said Mojo, forging a path through the stream of passers-by and taking intermittent bites out of a chocolate bar, "obviously what we need first is some gigs, right? – experience playing live."

Lauren was almost jogging to keep up with him. She shook her head. "Wrong. What we need first is a cup of coffee. Where is this totally *a*-mazing café of yours, anyway?"

"Just up here on the left." Mojo pointed to a set of display windows full of glowering mannequins in avant-garde fashions. Above the windows in bright pink neon glowed the words "Hyper Hyper".

"But this is a clothes store?" said Lauren.

"Aha," replied Mojo mysteriously. "That's what *you* think," and taking her arm he led the way through a pair of heavy swing doors.

On the other side Lauren found herself in a bustling, high-tech bazaar staffed by stallholders with extreme hair-cuts. What they were selling ranged from PVC dresses and day-glo jewellery to crinolines and leopard-skin pill-box hats. A tinkling electronic backtrack completed the atmosphere. "Well, Marks & Spencers it isn't," Lauren murmured, unzipping her down jacket and looking round in amazement.

Mojo cackled delightedly. "Marks & Spencers it isn't," he repeated. "You crease me up, Lauren – you know that? Come on, it's down here." Striding through the rows of designer creations he waved briefly to a very beautiful black girl selling shoes. She returned the wave and blew him a kiss. "That's Alex," Mojo explained.

"She's gorgeous," Lauren replied.

"Yeah, well – I can't help it if I've got good taste, can I?"

They turned a corner and suddenly Mojo stopped. "Da – *dah*!" There in front of them was a converted railway carriage straight out of Sherlock Holmes. Inside it small tables with white tablecloths, cruets and menus had been arranged between the seats.

"The Pullman Restaurant," Mojo announced. "Fab, eh? Afternoon tea now being served – plus today's special – a free sticky bun for anyone who's just joined a band."

"I don't know why I bother putting Danish pastries in my mouth," said Lauren as their order arrived five minutes later. "It would be easier applying them straight to my thighs – you know? – cut out the middle man?" She broke off a forkful, ate it with evident pleasure and grinned. "Anyway – where were we?"

"Gigs."

"Oh, right – gigs. You were telling me about your friend Carlton."

"Yeah, well – Carlton reckons there's a vacant Sunday lunchtime spot at the Green Man – this pub up in Hampstead. The money's not much cop, but it's a start."

Lauren nodded. "We'd have to audition though, wouldn't we?"

" 'Course." Mojo took the unwanted maraschino cherry he was being offered.

"But that'll be a doddle. I mean it's obvious you pick things up really fast, and you're great at improvising, so it won't take long for the three of us to put a set together. Then what we do is we go along to this bloke who runs the Green Man, play him our three best numbers, blow his socks off and bingo! – the gig's ours."

Lauren put down her fork decisively. "Now *that's* what I like to see. Up front, go-for-it enthusiasm."

Mojo took a mouthful of coffee and leaned back with a knowing, luxuriant grin. A sign above his head said "First Class Passengers". "Got to be confident in this life, Lauren. I mean if *you* don't think you're a winner, why should anyone else?" He scratched his right ear reflectively. "Take my dad, right. Five years ago he was made redundant. Wallop. Just like that. Forty-seven and on the scrap-heap. But did he stay there? No. He stuck all his redundancy money into starting a mini-cab business. Now he's got fourteen cars and employs seventeen people. Confidence, see? That's what he had."

Lauren smiled. "I guess you must be a lot like him."

56

"Yeah – I am in some ways." Mojo absently brushed some crumbs off the table.

"But? Do I detect a 'but'?"

Mojo paused. "Well, let's just say we have our differences, too." He examined the salt cellar for a moment then went on. "See, my Dad's got this big thing about me going to university and getting loads of qualifications. He reckons that's the only way to be secure. 'Get a degree. Get a degree.' He's always on about it."

"But you'd rather quit school and go into the music business, right?"

She received a slow nod. "Yep. I've tried to tell him, Lauren – 'cos I respect the man, like I say. I've tried to explain, but he just can't see it. Accountancy? – yes. Professional music?" – he gave a thumbs down sign.

"And what does your Mom think?"

Mojo grinned. "Oh, you know what mums are like." He broke into an impersonation of his mother's lilting, Jamaican accent. 'Listen to your father, Maurice – what he's saying is only for your own good.' Anyway . . ." he pushed his empty plate aside. "We didn't come here to talk about all that. We're supposed to be celebrating you joining Nexus."

Lauren raised her cup in a toasting gesture. "Well, thank you kindly, sir." They both drank in silence for a moment, then Lauren rested her chin on a cupped palm reflectively. "Mojo," she said tentatively. "This is a change of subject, but there's something I've been meaning to ask you."

"Hmmm?"

"It's about Jake."

"The well-known artist's model who can't be with us on account of a sitting? Yes?"

"Well – not just about Jake. About Jake and Charlie."

"Ahhhh!" Mojo folded his arms and leaned forwards, a twinkle appearing in his eye. "Now I was going to

57

raise that subject myself."

"You were?"

"Hmmm."

Lauren gathered her thoughts. "You see, you're Jake's best friend, right? – so I thought maybe *you* might know just what's going on between those two. I mean whenever they're in the same room it's like . . ." she distorted her face into a silent mask of stretched horror. "Why is that? See, I feel caught in the middle – especially now if I'm going to be seeing you guys regularly with the band. I told Charlie this morning I was just going to play a few tunes with the two of you and she looked at me like I had 'TRAITOR' tattooed on my forehead." There was a short, despondent pause. "And then there's this crazy journalism feud. That's how it all started, I guess. And now every time anyone so much as mentions the *Portobello Post*, Charlie turns into . . . into . . ." she searched for a suitable comparison ". . . Queen Victoria. You know? . . . 'We are *not* amused'."

Mojo chuckled appreciatively. "Well, if you want my opinion – are you ready for this? – I think Jake has a thing for Charlie but he's afraid to admit it. Don't look like that, it's true. That's what I was going to talk to you about – check out if you thought Charlie might feel the same way."

Lauren looked at him in blank astonishment. "Are you *serious*?"

" 'Course," said Mojo. "All that electricity. Got to come from somewhere, hasn't it? Classic love/hate relationship." He drained the last of his coffee while Lauren gave him a sidelong glance and raised one very doubtful eyebrow.

"Uh-uh. I think you're way off," she finally said. "It looks more like a good old-fashioned personality clash from where I'm standing. Anyway, wherever it comes from I wish it would go back there. Frankly, living with Queen Victoria is not my idea of a good time."

"Is it anybody's?" Mojo enquired.

Lauren smiled in spite of herself. "And you and Lindsey are no help," she want on, wagging a not very serious finger across the table. "Are you going to tell me that's a love/hate relationship, too?"

Mojo shook his head. "No – that's different. We just can't stand each other."

Lauren buried her head in her hands. "Honestly – all four of you are behaving like small children." She put on a petulant little girl voice. " 'My paper's going to be better than your paper.' I mean – *pulleease!*" They both laughed, Lauren in exasperation, Mojo with unadulterated glee, then Lauren noticed a clock on the far wall of the carriage.

"Is that the time? I've got to go. I'm supposed to be meeting Charlie and her mother outside the Albert Hall at 6.45." Mojo leaned sideways, caught the waiter's eye and made a scribbling gesture in the air.

"So what's happening at the Albert Hall?" he asked.

"Mahler's first symphony," replied Lauren nonchalantly. "Impressed?"

Mojo sniffed and drew down the corners of his mouth. "Nah," he lied.

Outside it was almost dark and a cold wind was blowing. "Well," said Lauren, pulling on her gloves. "Thanks for the Danish . . . and listen, I'm really excited about being in Nexus. I think we're going to have a lot of fun."

"Even if it means living with Queen Victoria?"

Lauren laughed. "I guess I'll survive," she said. "But anyway, will you ask Jake to at least *try* and be nice to her from now on?"

Mojo was stamping his feet to keep warm. "No harm in asking," he replied.

Lauren looked at the passing traffic for a moment. "See, I just want us to be friends."

"But we are friends."

59

"Not you and me, dummy. Jake and Charlie. I want all of us to be friends."

"Ahhhh," said Mojo, with his head on one side. "Sweet."

Lauren grinned and rolled her eyes to heaven in despair. "Give me a break," she muttered. Then, zipping up her jacket she turned, gave a brief wave and disappeared into the crowd.

Two minutes later Lauren was walking along Kensington Gore oblivious to both Hyde Park on one side and a four-lane traffic jam on the other. Lost in thought, she was sifting the contents of her new life in London. "London." Just the word had always seemed so exciting, even when she was a kid. Not in a dumb, Charles Dickensy way either, but *really* exciting. It was the one place she'd always dreamed of visiting and now here she was, with a new home, new friends like Mojo, a new school, Nexus . . . in fact things couldn't be going better. She glanced up at the dusty, burnished leaves of a copper beech and softly mouthed the words out loud as if they were a protective mantra – "Things couldn't be going better. Honestly, things just couldn't be going . . ." It was no use, though. Even as she spoke, a wave of pure, aching homesickness welled up from somewhere deep inside, broke, and washed over her. It was a sensation that had been happening every day for the last six weeks and it showed no signs of weakening. She swallowed hard and angrily quickened her step. OK, OK so she had bouts of homesickness. Big deal. She could handle it. She'd have to. There was absolutely no way she was going to wreck a perfectly good year in England by dwelling on it and whining like some spoiled brat. Anyway, Kyle was coming over in a couple of weeks – that would help. She felt reassured and made herself think about Kyle again. Yeah – that would help a lot.

By this time the Albert Hall was just across the road.

Standing at a set of traffic lights Lauren scanned the milling knots of concert-goers. Entrance D, they'd said. Entrance A . . . Entrance B . . . She spotted Charlie and her mother just as the lights changed. All right, enough is enough, she told herself, breaking into a broad grin and waving. They mustn't suspect. Sooner or later she'd settle in and stop feeling this way, but until then, nobody must suspect.

"So you are going to have a sports section, then?" asked Dave Anderson. It was the next day and Dave, along with Jake, Aftab, Brendan and the rest of the Portobello swimming team, was getting changed at Kensington New Pools.

Jake unbuttoned his shirt and stuffed it into a locker. "Yeah," he replied. "That's going to be half of the back p . . ."

"All right, all right," boomed a voice on the other side of the changing room. "Less chat, if you don't mind, gentlemen. This isn't a sewing circle, Shepherd."

"No sir," replied Jake.

"Get a move on, then."

"So what are you putting in the *rest* of the *Post*?" asked Brendan once Vic Drake, the burly, crew-cutted owner of the voice had passed out of earshot. "I've heard the *Gazette*'s running a photo of Mr Hammond with his wife and their new baby. Have *you* come up with any scoops?"

"Maybe – maybe not," answered Jake, fishing in the bottom of his sports bag for a pair of goggles. Dave looked left and right with a conspiratorial air then sat down abruptly between Jake and Brendan, his eyes shining. "Mojo reckons you've got a really big news story – something about the college. Is that right?" Jake was just about to answer when the changing room door burst open.

61

"I thought I said get a *move* on!"

"Coming, sir," said Brendan, bobbing up nervously and removing his glasses with both hands. The door closed.

"What is it about Vic that always makes me think of a brain-damaged gorilla?" asked Dave pensively.

"How unfair," sniggered Brendan.

"Especially to brain-damaged gorillas," added Jake, closing his locker door.

Dave and Jake resumed their conversation at the far end of the pool from Vic Drake twenty minutes later. They were sitting wrapped in large towels, waiting for their respective legs of a relay race to begin. "So anyway," Dave began over a barrage of cheers from around the vaulted, chlorine-smelling building. "Is it true, then? – about this 'big news' story?"

Jake drew both knees up to his chest. "Maybe."

"How did you find out about it?" There was no reply. "Oh, come on, Jake, what do you think I'm going to do, tell Cormack and Jordan?"

Jake rubbed his nose and sniffed. "No, I suppose not, but I still can't tell you how we got hold of it. Let's just say the information came our way, all right?"

Dave was beginning to shiver. He wrapped his towel closer round him. "Blimey. Sounds like you've got a 'Deep Throat' or something. Who is it?"

"Pass."

"Eh?"

"Mastermind, you daft wazzock."

"Oh, yeah." The conversation stopped for a moment while Dave and Jake both turned their attention to the pool.

"Come on, Aftab!" yelled Jake.

Dave leaned forwards and ran both hands through his peroxide bristles. "Could be a bit risky, though, couldn't it? I mean, what if this information of yours turns out to be wrong? Then you'd really be in the sh . . ."

"Dave," interrupted Jake forcefully. "The story's accurate and we're putting it in the *Post*. News is news, OK? People have a right to know the truth. That's all we're doing – letting them know the truth. End of chat."

"Yeah but . . ."

"Come on, it's us." The third pair of relay swimmers had just set off from the far end of the pool. Jake and Dave were the fourth. Standing up and shaking out his legs, Jake moved to the edge of the water and got into position – head down, knees bent – arms stretched out. Beside him Dave took up the same stance. The two swimmers coming towards them were neck and neck. Jake took three breaths in quick succession, adjusted his goggles, glanced across at Dave, crouched even lower, then, just as the swimmer below him touched the wall, pushed out and forward into space.

Back in the changing room Aftab was gelling his hair into a rockabilly DA when Jake got out of the shower. "What a team, eh?" he said to Jake's reflection as it walked past. Meanwhile, Dave was leaning, elbows locked, head down, on the next washbasin.

"I've got to stop smoking," he mumbled in the direction of the plughole. At that moment the changing room door burst open and there was a shrill whistle blast.

"The minibus leaves in five minutes," announced Vic Drake. "Think you can finish your coiffure in that time, Jehar?"

"Yes sir. Hope so, sir," replied Aftab.

As the door closed Brendan turned round. "Jake, have you got any deodorant? I seem to have forgotten mine."

"Yeah – in my bag. Help yourself," replied Jake, rapidly pulling on a sock which once in its life had been white. Brendan rummaged around in Jake's sports bag for a few seconds, then his hands suddenly came to a halt. "What are these?" he asked holding up two rolls of film.

"Oh those," replied Jake casually, feeling his throat constrict. "Nothing. Just some photos a mate of Mojo's took for the *Post*. I'm supposed to be developing them after school in the dark room."

He held out his hand, but Brendan had noticed something scribbled on the casing of one of the rolls in black felt-tip pen.

"What's this say?" he enquired innocently. "D. .E. .S. .I. .R. ."

"Brendan, give me the . . ."

"Terrible writing. Is that last letter an 'E'? Or else I suppose it coul . . ."

Jake stood up, snatched the rolls of film and abruptly sat down again. Brendan stared at him with his mouth slightly open.

"Sorry," he said weakly. "I was only . . ."

"That's OK," replied Jake, with a feeble attempt at a conciliatory smile. "I just don't want everybody knowing what's in the *Post* before it's even printed, that's all." There was a slightly uncomfortable silence during which Dave and Aftab exchanged a puzzled look.

"Desire?" said Dave. "I don't get it. What's that got t . . ." Suddenly his face broke into a broad grin. "Hang on. It's not 'desire'. It's Desirée – Desirée Montgomery. Mojo's always on about what a great Page Three girl she'd make. Is that what those are? Page Three photos of Desirée Montgomery? Eh?" He looked at Jake for confirmation and got it in the form of several rapid blinks and a tightening of the lips. "Tsk, tsk, tsk," said Dave, pretending to disapprove. "Smutty boys. I wonder what Charlie and Lindsey would say if they knew about *that*!"

Chapter 5

Charles Johnson stood in the doorway of his son's bed-room wearing a look of deep disapproval. "Maurice – it's 8.45." He was addressing a large lump hidden by bedclothes. The lump didn't respond. *"Maurice!"* This time the lump began to stir. "If you don't get up right now you'll be late for school again. Do you hear me?"

"All right. All right," said a muffled voice from some-where under the duvet. Mojo's father scanned the music magazines and record covers scattered around his son's room for a moment. Then, with one final granite stare at the bed which somehow managed to combine anger and sadness, he turned and left.

Downstairs in the Johnson's kitchen, eight-year-old Phoebe was dunking an egg soldier with great concentra-tion when her older brother shuffled into the room two minutes later. "What's the matter with *you*?" she asked, putting down the soldier. "Your eyes are all icky."

"Phoebe, eat your breakfast," said Charles, from be-hind his newspaper.

Mojo stuck out his tongue at Phoebe, carefully sat down and poured himself a cup of coffee, mumbling "Hi, Mum" as he did so. Across the room Eugenia Johnson turned from the stove with a wooden spatula in one hand.

"Well good morning," she replied, and was about to go on frying bacon when she noticed what Phoebe had remarked on a few moments earlier. Placing one hand on her hip, she frowned. "Maurice, you look terrible."

"Thanks," said Mojo, reaching for a slice of toast.

Charles lowered the *Daily Mail* and took off his glasses. "What time did you get in last night?"

"I dunno – twelve – half past," replied Mojo.

"Try twenty past two," his father corrected.

Mojo carried on buttering the piece of toast on his plate. "OK, so it was later than I thought." He paused and cleared his throat. "You know how it is when you're working on something and lose track of time." He tried to will an enthusiastic expression onto his face. "But honestly, Dad, this newspaper project I'm doing with Jake is going *so well* . . ."

"Only you weren't really with Jake last night, were you?" said Charles.

Phoebe was watching her father carefully. Now she put down the glass of orange juice she had been holding with both hands, straightened her back and turned to Mojo, who was smiling incredulously.

"Eh? What are you on about? 'Course I was. I told you that's where I was going, remember?"

Charles Johnson got up, walked into the hall and came back a few seconds later carrying an olive-green flying jacket. "Your friend Carlton came by about twenty minutes ago and dropped this off."

"Oh, is that who was at the door?" remarked Eugenia. Charles, who hadn't taken his eyes off Mojo's face, waited a second before going on.

"He said you left it at the club last night. I said 'What club?' and he said 'The Jamboree Bag' . . . where you've been working two nights a week for the last month."

Mojo put down the piece of toast that was half way to his mouth. Somewhere in the background an old Beatles song – "Please, Please Me" – was playing on the radio. For a second nobody spoke, then apparently Mojo decided he had nothing to lose. "Well, what if I am?" he began defiantly. "What's wrong with that?"

"I'll tell you exactly what's wrong with it." Charles Johnson's voice was very low and very calm. "In the first place you're under age to work in a nightclub – in the second place it's making you too tired to do anything but sleep at school – and in the third place . . ." his voice fell even lower, ". . . you lied about it to your mother and me."

Mojo looked up quickly, his eyes flashing with indignation. "Only because I knew you'd go apeshit if I told you the truth."

"Maurice!" said Eugenia angrily. She turned to Phoebe. "Go upstairs and clean your teeth."

"But I want to see what happens."

"Phoebe," Eugenia repeated. "Just do as I say." Reluctantly Phoebe slid off her chair and left the room. As she did so Mojo looked at his watch. "Can we talk about this later? It's nine o'clock. I've got to go to school."

"No, we cannot talk about it later. We are going to tal . . ."

Eugenia Johnson laid a pacifying hand on her husband's arm. "All right," he said after a short pause. "I suppose it can wait until tonight." He leaned forwards, ". . . but let me make one thing perfectly clear. As of today, this job of yours *stops*. Understand?" Mojo pushed back his chair without answering and stood up.

"Aren't you going to finish your breakfast?" asked Eugenia. "I was frying some bacon for you."

"No thanks," replied Mojo. "I just lost my appetite."

"Well, I'm *not* giving up working at 'The Jamboree Bag', and if he thinks I am he's got another think coming," said Mojo angrily, as he and Jake walked through the gates of Portobello ten minutes later.

"But how can you carry on now your old man's found out about it?" asked Jake.

"I don't know." The muscles in Mojo's jaw were set. "But I'll think of something."

"Yeah, well I'd think of telling Carlton he's a right

67

wally if I was you," Jake went on. "I mean what a div, rolling up and giving the jacket to your Dad."

Mojo waved the topic away as they entered the main building. "I don't even want to think about it." He walked on in silence for a few stops, then suddenly brightened. "Come on, cheer me up. Tell me how the photos of Desirée came out."

Jake swung his briefcase over one shoulder and took a deep breath. "What can I say? I mean, they're amazing."

"Do you mean the photos, or Desirée's . . ."

Jake sighed. "Give it a rest! You know what I . . ."

"Shtum! Here comes Jordan." Lindsey Jordan had just turned a corner with a group of three other girls and was walking down the corridor towards them.

"Morning," said Jake pleasantly as she drew level. Lindsey arranged her lips into the smallest possible gesture of polite recognition and walked by.

"So anyway," Mojo continued. "Where are they? – the photos I mean. Have you got them here?"

"Yeah." Jake stopped beside the school noticeboard and began tying up a loose shoelace. "They're in my bag."

"Let's have a look, then."

"Not now!" Jake looked up at Mojo's eager face. "After Music, all right? But listen, I'm still not convinced it's a good . . ."

"Jake. Maurice. I'd like to see you in my room right away, please."

Mojo wheeled round and saw Phil Hammond standing behind them. "But we've got Music now, sir."

"That's all right. I've told Mr Brand you'll be a few minutes late."

Jake and Mojo exchanged a fleeting glance. "What's going on?" mouthed Mojo. Jake shrugged his shoulders, then together they followed Phil down the corridor and into Room 28.

"Close the door behind you," said Phil. He moved to

his desk, sat down, took out a large, buff envelope and tapped it lightly on the palm of his left hand. "When I arrived today this was on my desk," he began.

"What is it, sir?" asked Jake as an uncomfortable possibility dawned on him.

"You tell me." Phil emptied out the contents of the envelope and Jake's fears were confirmed. There, grinning up at him, was the face, and a good deal more, of Desirée Montgomery. Beside the photograph was a typewritten note which read "Ban the **Porn**obello *Post*". It was unsigned. "Well?" said Phil, after a brief silence during which Mojo breathed in and out heavily through his nose and Jake frowned at the floor. "Would either of you care to tell me what all this is about?"

"Censorship – that's what it is!" fumed Mojo during the morning break when he and Jake finally got a chance to talk. Slumped morosely in a corner seat of the students' cafeteria he was breaking a polystyrene cup into very small pieces. "I mean," he went on indignantly, "what gives him the right to say we can't have a Page Three girl in the *Post*?"

"He's in charge of the course, you nerk, that's what gives him the right," replied Jake.

Mojo snorted derisively. "Yeah well – so much for all that twaddle he gave us the other day about 'full editorial control'. 'Full editorial control' – huh!" He cupped his chin in both hands and stared darkly out of the window for a second before resuming, even more wound up than before. "And saying we can't print it because old Busby would have a seizure. I mean, what's that got to do with anything? We're talking about the freedom of the press here, aren't we?" Jake didn't respond. "I say we're talking about . . ."

"The telephone call!" Jake suddenly exclaimed, coming out of a brief reverie. "Of course!"

69

Mojo looked perplexed. "What telephone call?" Jake leaned forwards. "I've just worked out how that photo got onto Hammond's desk. Yesterday when I was in the dark-room Angela Mogridge knocked on the door about half past four and said there was a phone call for me."

"So?"

"Well, I thought it was pretty strange – who'd phone me at school? Anyway, I went, but when I got there the line was dead." He leaned back and shook his head in disbelief. "What a prat. I should have known."

"What? Known *what*?" demanded Mojo, still looking perplexed.

Jake quickly told him about Brendan finding the films in his sports bag the previous day and Dave's joking threat to tell Charlie and Lindsey. "I thought he was just messing about, but obviously he *did* tell Cormack and Jordan. So after school one of them phoned Mogridge's office and got me out of the way while the other one sneaked into the dark room. There were loads of prints, so I didn't even notice one of them had gone. Then they wrote an anonymous note, bunged it in an envelope and stuck the whole lot on Hammond's desk."

"Revenge for that business at Cormack's house, you mean?" said Mojo.

Jake nodded. "Too right," he agreed.

At that moment Lauren and Charlie walked into the cafeteria laughing happily. Lauren spotted Jake and Mojo, waved, then turned to Charlie and whispered something in her ear. At first Charlie seemed dubious about whatever it was Lauren had said, but eventually nodded and with a small push in the back began making her way across the room. Lauren followed a few steps behind, grinning. "They're coming over," hissed Jake. "Leave this to me, all right? I'll do all the talking."

"Well, hello," began Lauren breezily as she and Charlie reached the table. "How's it going? Mind if we join you?"

"No – go ahead," said Jake, looking expressionlessly at Charlie. "I think we're due to have a little chat, don't you?"

"Oh good," broke in Lauren, casting a significant sideways glance at Mojo. "I was just saying to Charlie – wasn't I, Charlie? – how nice it would be if we could all just have a . . . friendly . . . cup . . . of" she fell silent, realizing from Jake and Mojo's icy expressions that a friendly cup of coffee wasn't what they had in mind. Charlie had obviously made the same observation.

"Is anything wrong?" she asked, lifting a lock of hair behind her ear with one finger.

"I think you know exactly what's wrong," replied Jake.

"Do I?"

"Yes."

Charlie shook her head and smiled. "I'm sorry, but— "

"Well, if you think it's going to end there you're making a big mistake," Jake went on. "Because let's get one thing clear. What I did and what you did are *not* in the same league."

"Wait a minute." Charlie's face was beginning to register disapproval. "What exactly are you accus— "

"And with or without Desirée Montgomery— "

"Desirée *who*?" asked Lauren.

Charlie stood up. "Listen," she said, her eyes flashing. "I don't know what's going on here, but obviously you think I've done something to harm your precious scandal sheet. Well, I haven't."

"I don't believe you," replied Jake.

"Are you calling me a liar?"

"Absolutely."

"Then say it."

"You're a liar."

"Right."

"Guys," interrupted Lauren. "Could you both please— " but before she was able to finish, Charlie had picked up her books and stalked away. "Great," said

71

Lauren, wearily hoisting a duffle bag over one shoulder and forming an "O" with the index finger and thumb of one hand. Her voice was shaky. "Really terrific. Thanks a bunch." And with that she stood up and followed the departing figure of Charlie across the cafeteria.

"More mulled wine, darling?" Gudrun Cormack held out a large, steaming jug as another firework exploded in the sky over Holland Park. For a second it threw her full-length fur coat and baggy suede boots into silhouette, then shimmered and cascaded into blackness.

"Thanks," replied Charlie, shouting to make herself heard. She watched as the hot, red stream filled her plastic cup, smiled by way of thanks, then turned back to the bonfire. It was a still, frosty evening and the communal gardens behind Briardale Crescent were crowded with shrieking, sparkler-waving children and their parents. Charlie showed no interest in the people round her, though. In fact, once Gudrun had moved on she became totally absorbed in watching the bonfire.

"Hello, C."

"Hmmm? Oh, Dad! Hello." Charlie smiled as her father appeared out of the crowd.

"You looked miles away just now," said Antony Cormack. "What were you thinking about?" Charlie snuggled happily against the lapel of his coat.

"Actually I was thinking about that fireworks party we had a few years ago in California. Remember?"

Antony chuckled. "Behind the house in Berkeley, you mean? All I remember is your mother making me fish dead Catherine wheels out of the pool at some ungodly hour the next morning." They both laughed, then Antony took a mouthful of mulled wine and looked at the spiral of sparks rising from the bonfire. "Seems a long time ago, doesn't it – California?"

Charlie sighed a cloud of frosty air. "Sometimes. It's

amazing how much having Lauren around brings it all back, though."

"Where is Lauren by the way?" asked Antony, looking round. "I thought she just had a few letters to write, then she was coming down."

Charlie turned up the collar of her coat. "I don't really think she's in the mood for a party. Not after that phone call from Kyle's parents yesterday. She was so looking forward to him coming over next week."

Antony nodded as another rocket went screeching into the night sky. "He will be all right, though, won't he? This motorbike accident he's had isn't serious?"

"No, I don't think so. Severe bruising and a broken leg – that's what they said."

"Nasty all the same." Antony picked a clove out of his wine and threw it onto the fire. "Poor old Lauren. Just as she was really settling in." Father and daughter stood in silence for a moment watching the firelit scene, then Antony squeezed Charlie's shoulder affectionately and turned towards her. "Talking of people settling in – what about you? We haven't had time for a proper chat recently, have we?"

"No."

"How's school and everything?"

"Oh" – Charlie moved her weight from one foot to the other. "You know – all right."

"Only all right?"

"Well, the courses and the teachers are fine, but some of the kids are a bit immature." She paused. "In fact one or two are extremely immature, come to think of it. Apart from that, though . . ."

"No regrets about leaving Dartington, then?"

Charlie shook her head. "Heavens, no. I'm really glad we came to London. Honestly."

"Good." Antony took a swig of mulled wine, allowing the warm liquid to roll around his palate before he swallowed it. "And how's Julian?" he enquired. "I'm surprised we haven't seen more of him now the two of you are only forty miles apart. Everything still all right in that department?"

Charlie averted her eyes. "Yes. Of course. Actually I went up to Oxford last weekend when you were in Paris. Didn't Mummy tell you?"

"Ah – now you mention it, I think she did," Antony replied.

"He's working terribly hard."

"Well, I suppose he'd have to be. Finals next summer, after all. God, I remember staying up for nights on end when I did mine."

Charlie gave her full attention to a black, wizened sparkler on the muddy ground.

"Hmmm," she agreed noncommittally, adding after a moment's thought: "A person can work *too* hard, though."

Antony allowed a moment to pass, then cleared his throat. "Is that remark directed at me as well as Julian, by any chance?" Charlie looked into her father's face and made a small apologetic grimace, confirming his suspicion. "Yes, well – point taken," he began. "I know I've been away more than usual since we moved up here, but it's this damned Strelson takeover thing. You know how important it is to the company, C. The chairman's on my back about it all the damned time and I've just had to give it 101%. You understand, don't you, darling?"

"Yes, of course," said Charlie, pulling a loose thread from her scarf. "But— "

"But you'll be glad when it's over and the old man starts spending more time at home like an ordinary human being again."

"Something like that."

Antony took a deep breath of night air. "Well, that makes two of us." He hesitated, then seemed to take a decision. "Oh, well, it's not official yet, but you may as well know." He grasped Charlie's hands in his own. "The rumour is we should have a majority of shareholders on our side by early December."

Charlie turned and examined her father's eyes carefully. "And when that happens does it mean the deal's complete?"

"Well, no, not technically, not absolutely . . . but it certainly means the worst will be over and I might be able to take a bit of time off."

Relief flooded into Charlie's face. She hugged her father then suddenly stood back, her eyes wide and shining. "I've just had an idea," she said excitedly. "Why don't we all go away somewhere?"

"Away?"

"Yes. On holiday." Charlie pressed gloved hands to her cheeks. "Christmas abroad. Oh, it would be great. I mean, we've all earned a break, haven't we? And it's just what Lauren needs, too." She waited eagerly for a reaction.

"Well, I suppose we could," Antony mused. "I mean, barring last-minute hitches." A flicker of doubt tightened the lines around his eyes, then passed. "Oh, the hell with it – why not? We'll go to Austria – do a bit of skiing in Kitzbühl."

"Oh Dad, do you mean it?"

" 'Course I mean it. Don't you trust your old man?"

Charlie kissed him on the cheek. Then, pressing her half-empty cup into his hands she turned and began running across the frosty garden.

"Hey! Where are you going?" Antony called after her.

"To tell Lauren," Charlie shouted over one shoulder.

Antony chuckled affectionately as he watched his daughter's figure recede into the darkness beyond the fireworks party. For the first time in weeks he felt completely happy and relaxed. The sensation was short-lived, though. Turning back to the bonfire his expression slowly began to change, and in a matter of only a few seconds he was lost in deep, uneasy thought. Had he done the right thing saying they could go away? True, the Strelson deal seemed to be in the bag, but what if it wasn't? What if it all went sour? What if . . . He ran a hand across his face and noticed with alarm that in spite of the cold evening his forehead was damp with perspiration.

As she climbed the stepladder to Lauren's room, Charlie could hear a muffled Bruce Springsteen song on the other side of the trapdoor. She knocked. "Anyone home?"

"Wait a second," was the reply, then a few moments later, "OK, come on in." Lauren was sitting cross-legged under the triangular attic window writing on an airmail pad. Several scrunched-up sheets of pale blue paper were on the floor beside her. "You're back early," she said, turning down the cassette recorder. "I was just going to come down."

"Listen, listen," interrupted Charlie, sitting on the bed. "I've got the most wonderful news." She was still breathing hard after running all the way from the fireworks party.

"Oh yeah?" Lauren put one hand against the small of her back and stretched. "I could use some. What is it?" Quickly Charlie explained.

"Austria!" said Lauren.

"That's right," beamed Charlie. "Won't it be great?" She searched Lauren's face but didn't find the expected reaction. "What's wrong?" she asked finally. "I thought you'd be excited."

Lauren gently shook her head. "I can't go to Austria," she murmured.

"Why not?"

"Because . . . well, for one thing I can't afford it."

Charlie pulled a face. "Don't worry about that. Think of all the places you and your parents took *me* to see when I was in America."

"That was different." Lauren turned off the anglepoise

beside her. "I mean a weekend camping trip in Yosemite isn't exactly the same as a skiing holiday in the Tyrol, is it? Besides— "

"Besides what?" Charlie folded her arms as Bruce Springsteen sang about cars, turnpikes and escape in the background. "Oh, I get it. You think we're just organizing this holiday to make up for Kyle not coming over – is that it?"

Lauren paused, picked up a cushion and held it against her stomach defensively. "Yeah. Kinda looks that way." She saw Charlie's face fall. "God, I must sound so ungrateful and I'm *not*, really. It's just . . . well . . . I can't think about having fun on some alp somewhere right now – that's all – not with Kyle . . ." she broke off and frowned at the carpet.

Charlie bit her bottom lip. "No, of course not." She climbed off the bed and sat next to Lauren on the floor. "And of course you're worried now – but honestly, every-thing will look different in a few days, I'm sure. Kyle's parents said he wasn't hurt very badly, so he'll probably be out of hospital in two or three . . ."

"No, he won't. He'll be in there at least a month," interrupted Lauren, pulling the cushion closer to her chin and taking a series of shallow breaths.

Charlie leaned back with a bewildered expression on her face. "How do you know that?" she asked.

"Because I spoke to Kyle's best friend, Mike Piatroni, a few hours ago – just after you guys went out." Lauren looked up and tried to smile. "Don't worry – I called collect." She averted her eyes again and made a grasping gesture with both fists as if she was trying to explain something very important. "See, when Kyle's mother called yesterday I knew, I could just tell from her voice that she wasn't being straight with me. I kept asking questions and all I got was this brittle, chipper, optimistic little voice telling me how every-thing was perfectly under control." She sniffed and rubbed the end of her nose. "Anyway, Mike told me the truth."

"And what is the truth?"

"That Kyle's screwed-up his back really badly. He's in traction and . . . and he needed forty-eight . . . forty-eight sti . . ." she put one hand across her mouth and began, soundlessly at first, to cry.

Moving closer, Charlie put an arm round her friend's shoulder. "It's all right," she whispered. "It's all right. Ssshhh. Everything's going to be all right."

For a minute neither of the girls spoke, then finally Lauren's crying stopped in several long, juddering gasps. Pulling a tissue out of a box on the floor she blew her nose loudly, turned red-eyed to Charlie and gave her a more successful smile. "Totally gorgeous, right?" she asked.

Charlie laughed softly. "Do you want an honest answer?"

Lauren quickly held up a prohibiting palm. "No thanks." She blew her nose again. "Look, I'm really sorry. This was the one thing I promised myself I wouldn't do. It's just . . . I wanted to see him *so bad* and now . . ."

"Do you think perhaps you should go home for a while?" asked Charlie. "I mean if you do I'm sure we could . . ."

"I don't know what I want." Lauren shrugged. "One minute I think I'm over-reacting to the whole situation, next minute I see him lying in a hospital bed totally helpless while I'm here on the other side of the world."

Charlie nodded and stroked Lauren's hair. "Well, you don't have to make your mind up right away. Why don't you phone again tomorrow and see how he is? You know, take it one day at a time."

Lauren squeezed her eyes tight shut and opened them again. "Yeah, you're right," she said, hugging her knees.

"Besides, what could I do even if I *did* fly home straight away?" She tried out a shakily optimistic smile. OK, I feel better now."

"Really?"

"Really. Come on, let's talk about something else." There was an A4 pad lying on the bedside table. Reaching over, Lauren picked it up. "I was going to show you this. It's the . . . uh . . . it's that piece you asked me to do for the *Gazette* – you know? 'A Yank at Portobello'?"

"Oh, can I see?" asked Charlie.

"Sure – here you go. But it's only a first draft. I was going to tighten it up tomorrow." Charlie scanned the first paragraph while Lauren, realizing that Bruce Springsteen had finished, blew her nose again and pressed the eject button on her cassette recorder. Suddenly the telephone downstairs began to ring. "Listen, why don't you take that with you and let me have it back in the morning?" said Lauren. "Cos I think I'm going to turn in now."

Charlie glanced at her watch. "But it's only half past nine."

"I know. I just feel like an early night, that's all."

Charlie shrugged, moved to the trapdoor and stopped with her foot on the top step. "No lying awake worrying, though – all right?"

Lauren smiled. "Absolutely not. Oh, Charlie – one more thing. Will you do me a favour?"

"What?"

"Don't tell the kids at school about Kyle, OK? I'd just as soon handle this on my own."

On an impulse Jake suddenly jumped up and shouted at the top of his voice, "Look out, world – Nexus is coming to get you!" Then he waved an invisible football scarf above his head, gave two protracted whoops and sat down again next to a surprised-looking Mojo. They were sharing a bench at the top of Parliament Hill, below which London sprawled and stretched in weak November sunshine. Mojo turned up his collar, trying not to laugh as an old lady walking a spaniel glowered at

Jake's behaviour. Elsewhere two grim-faced joggers and a father and son flying kites were the only other people in view.

"Finished?" Mojo enquired. Jake turned and shook him enthusiastically by the shoulders. "We did it, Mo – we actually did it! We got the job!"

"I know." Mojo waited for the shaking to stop. "I was there, remember?" but Jake wasn't listening.

"Ruddy marvellous," he went on, releasing Mojo and swivelling back to face the toy-town version of the capital spread beneath them. "That's what we were today – just numero uno totally brillo-pad ruddy marvellous."

"Look, come off the fence," Mojo smiled. "Do you think the audition went well or don't you?" They both laughed, then fell into a companionable silence for a few seconds, a silence which Mojo finally broke. "Shame Lauren had to go off straight away."

"Hmmm," Jake agreed. "Do you think . . .?" he began, but seemed to change his mind about what he'd been going to say.

"What?"

"Nothing. She just seemed a bit strange today. Not at 'The Green Man' or anything – afterwards, I mean. She hardly said a word."

Mojo crossed his ankles. "I expect it's to do with that bust-up you and Charlie had the other day."

Jake folded his arms. "Meaning what?"

"Well, look at it from Lauren's point of view," Mojo went on. "Here she is in Nexus, and now all of a sudden we've got a regular pub gig, right? – so she's going to be spending a lot of time with us. Meanwhile her best mate reckons you're public enemy number one. Can't be easy, can it?"

"Hang on, hang on," Jake twisted round indignantly. "Are you defending Cormack here? Whose side are you on, exactly?"

"Yours, you great pranny!" said Mojo impatiently.

"I'm just trying to point out why Lauren might act a bit . . . strange . . . on account of the crossfire, that's all."

"Well, let me know when your Nobel Peace Prize arrives, won't you?"

"Right."

"Good."

"Sarky git." Jake turned his attention to the tail of a ripped kite caught in a tree.

"I still think you fancy her," Mojo said finally.

"Who?"

"Who'd you think?"

Jake gave his friend a withering glance, sniffed self-consciously and focussed on the Post Office Tower. "So anyway," he began, changing the subject. "What's happening about 'The Jamboree Bag'? Are you chucking it or what?"

Mojo groaned and leaned forwards. "Yeah. Dad made me phone Carlton yesterday and say I couldn't do it any more." He sighed. "Old fart. Still – could have been worse. I mean it was only a temporary thing from the word go. I was supposed to stop in a few weeks anyway."

Something suddenly occurred to Jake. "Hold on. Your Dad's not going to make a fuss about you playing up here in Hampstead every Sunday, is he?"

Mojo shrugged his shoulders. "Dunno."

"You are going to tell him about it, aren't you?"

"Oh yeah!" Mojo confirmed, adding after a long pause ". . . eventually."

Jake looked dubious but decided not to press the subject. "What time is it?" he asked.

"Ten past three. Blimey! I'd better get a move on," said Mojo, leaning over to pick up his guitar case.

"What's the rush? I thought we were going back to my place to write up the staff-cuts article for the *Post*. I mean, you were the one who was all fired-up after you saw that report on Angela Mogridge's desk."

"Yeah, I know," Mojo replied sheepishly, "but we'll have to do that tomorrow. Didn't I tell you? Something sort of . . . cropped up last night."

Jake put on an "I should have known" face. "Which one is it this time?"

"Alex – I told you about her – the fashion designer?" Jake nodded. "Well, last night she called me up, right, and said she had to see me 'urgently' at half past four today. Apparently there's something she *really* wants to talk about." Mojo's eyebrows suggested he had a fair idea what the "something" might be.

"So naturally this Alex gets priority over the *Post*," said Jake, only half-pretending to look offended.

"Just for this afternoon – that's all," Mojo protested. It was starting to rain. "Come on," he said, standing up. "Race you to the bottom." At first Jake kept up his martyred expression, but it soon disappeared as he watched Mojo career down the hill, one arm flailing, the other gripping his guitar case.

"That's what I've always admired about you, Mo," he muttered, getting wearily to his feet. "Your maturity." Then, summoning up the loudest possible battle cry, he set off in pursuit.

When Jake got home half an hour later, his mother was lying on the living room sofa looking pensive in a faded silk dressing gown. There was a completely full, stone-cold cup of tea on the table beside her and a Joni Mitchell album on the record player. Jake walked in, took off his coat and flopped in an armchair. "Hi," he shouted above the music.

Kay visibly jumped. "Oh, Jake!" she said, and put a hand over her heart. Turning down the record player she glanced at the cheroot in her hand, realized it was no longer alight and stubbed it out.

"How did you get on?"

Jake breathed on the finger nails of one hand and buffed them proudly against his shirt.

"You got it! Oh, what a star! Come here." She stood up and gave Jake a big hug.

"Yeah, not bad, eh?" he remarked, taking his place in the armchair again. "Ten quid a week, every Sunday lunchtime between now and Christmas. You'll have to come and see us play next weekend" . . . he pulled his left earlobe and added, ". . . you and Graham, I mean."

"Hmmm," Kay nodded enthusiastically and ran both hands through her hair, noticing it was still damp from the bath. "Actually, I wanted to . . ."

"Is there any tea in the pot?" asked Jake.

"What? Oh, yes. I mean, there is but it's probably stewed by now. Why don't you make some fresh?"

"OK." Jake hauled himself out of the armchair and went into the kitchen whistling the tune of "What's Up?"

"How's your introduction for the catalogue coming on?" he called, filling up the kettle.

"Oh, all right," Kay answered. "You know me – slowly." While he waited for the water to boil, Jake went back to the living room and leaned in the open doorway.

"You all right, Mum?" he asked, frowning slightly. Kay had lit another cheroot. Normally she only smoked in the evenings.

"Yes – why?" she replied.

"I don't know. You seem a bit – on edge." He paused, then smiled reassuringly. "Honestly – you've got nothing to worry about – the exhibition's bound to be . . ."

"It's not that," Kay broke in abruptly. Then, in a softer voice, she added. "Come and sit down. There's something we need to talk about."

Puzzled, Jake crossed the room and sat down beside her. "What is it? Has anything happened?" he asked.

"In a way." Kay looked towards the fireplace and

gathered her thoughts before going on. "You know I went out with Graham last night."

"Yeah."

"Well, he took me to a French place in the Fulham Road – 'Le Jardin'."

"And?"

"And halfway through dinner we started having this . . . I don't know . . . this 'serious' conversation."

"What about?"

"Oh, all sorts of things." Jake changed position slightly before his mother went on: "Then on the way home he asked me a question."

"How do you mean?"

"Oh come on, sweetie, don't be dim. *The* question."

"I still . . . oh."

"Exactly. He asked me to marry him."

Chapter 6

"Mr Hammond, Headmaster."

"Philip. Good morning. Come in, come in." Tom Busby stood up and indicated the other chair in his office. Meanwhile Angela Mogridge closed the door behind Phil and marched back to her small, ultra-tidy room across the corridor.

"Now," she said, having watered the row of cactus plants on the window sill, "where's that report of Mr Crane's? – the head's going to need it for his meeting with the governors tonight." Donning her spectacles she rummaged through the pile of papers in her out tray, but without success. Frowning, she straightened up. "How very odd." Then she saw the report wedged halfway down the contents of her in tray. "Aha – there you are." Relieved, she pulled out a ring binder with "Staffing and Financing Proposals" written on the cover, but her meticulous sense of order had obviously been disturbed. Glancing back at the out tray she shook her head. "I really could have sworn . . ." she began, but unable to solve the little mystery she eventually shrugged and got on with some filing.

Back in Tom Busby's office, Phil was explaining why he'd asked for an early morning appointment. "It's about video recorders," he began and watched the welcoming gleam in Tom's eye rapidly begin to fade. "You see, Headmaster, since the Media Studies one finally broke down a few weeks ago we've had to share with the Geography department, which means . . ."

"The answer's no."

Phil looked taken aback. "But . . . you don't even know what I was going to . . ."

"Yes I do. You were going to ask me for £300 so the Media Studies department could have a new VCR all to itself. Am I right or am I wrong?"

"Well . . . right, I suppose," Phil admitted.

Tom folded his arms and nodded. "The fact is we haven't got the money – it's as simple as that."

Phil undid the top button of his shirt. "I don't think you quite understand, Headmaster. What we're talking about here isn't a luxury. It's a vital piece of Media Studies equipment."

Tom Busby grunted. "I assure you I do understand, but what *you* don't seem to realize is that my hands are tied. You see, Media Studies isn't a core curriculum subject, is it?"

Phil momentarily closed his eyes. "I'm well aware of that, but . . ."

"Then you should appreciate that with things being what they are, it can't expect to come top of the list for new resources."

"I'm not *asking* to be top of the list," Phil exclaimed. "I'm just asking for the basic raw materials to do my job!"

"Well, *my* job is to keep this school running as best I can with the money available," replied Tom Busby emphatically. "And that involves making choices – saying 'yes' to some things and 'no' to others." He opened his palms wide. "I'm sorry."

Phil drummed a brief tattoo on the arm of his chair. "And it's not worth me trying to change your mind?"

"No."

A moment later the two men were locked in eye contact as the nine o'clock bell went. "Right then, I'll be off," said Phil, standing up and moving towards the door. "Thank you for your time."

"Hammond's on his way," announced Mojo, strutting languidly into Room 28. He wove a path to the back of the room, dumped his bag on the desk next to Jake's and tapped him on the shoulder.

"What? Oh, hi." Jake pulled off his Walkman earphones and closed the *Daily Mirror*.

"Listen," Mojo hissed urgently. "I think I've got us a lead on a *big* cover story for the *Post*. Even bigger than the staff-cuts thing."

Jake shot a wary glance across the room to where Lindsey was sitting, but she was deep in conversation with Aftab, Dave and Brendan. "Go on," he murmured softly, shielding one side of his face and leaning forwards.

"Well, this Alex, right? – the one I met up with yesterday?"

"Yeah."

"She told me about three friends of hers who were in All Saints Road last Friday night when . . ."

"Good morning." Phil Hammond strode in and immediately started writing on the blackboard in a series of terse clicks and squeaks.

"Tell me later," hissed Jake. Mojo nodded.

"Now today," Phil swung around from the blackboard a few seconds later, jiggling a piece of chalk in his right hand, "I want to talk about . . ." He frowned, noticing two empty desks at the front of the room. "Where are Lauren and Charlotte? Anyone seen them?"

"No, sir," replied Lindsey, gazing into Phil's eyes with rapt attention.

"No, sir," mimicked Mojo silently from the back row, adding a final pout for good measure.

Phil glanced at his watch, clearly irritated. "Well, we'd better make a start anyway. OK, today we're going to look at ownership of the press." He sat on his desk. "A while ago you remember we covered editorial control – how much independence editors have or should have." At this point Jake directed a meaningful glance at Dave

Anderson, who looked bemused. "Well, behind the editor, of course, is the real boss – the paper's owner. All right – what I want to do first is simply make a list of who owns the major UK dailies so we know who we're talking about. The *Mirror*, for example." He pointed to the copy in front of Jake. "Who owns that?"

An hour later, as Phil left the room, Dave Anderson came over to Jake's desk. "Going to swimming practice tonight?" he asked. Jake continued putting books in his bag without looking up or replying. "Shep, I said are you going swimming?" Still getting no answer Dave frowned and shifted his weight from one foot to the other. "What's going on?" he grinned, turning to a stony-faced Mojo.

"You know full well what's going on," muttered Jake darkly.

"No, I don't."

"Oh yes, you do." Jake stood up and stared Dave straight in the eye. "You shopped Mojo and me to Cormack and Jordan."

"Eh?"

"Well, it may have been *your* idea of a joke, but it wasn't *mine*." Jake emphasized the last word by jabbing a finger into Dave's chest.

"Oi! Leave it out!" replied Dave, taking a step backwards. He seemed genuinely surprised and shaken. "I didn't tell anybody anything!"

Jake snorted derisively. "So how come one of the prints of Desirée Montgomery just happened to turn up on Hammond's desk then? Bit of a coincidence after the other day in the changing room, wouldn't you say?"

"But that was a joke! You don't seriously think I . . ."

The sound of a throat being vigorously cleared made Jake, Dave and Mojo all turn round. The only other person left in the room was Brendan, who lowered his hand, revealing a tense, determined expression. "Dave's quite right. He had nothing to do with stealing the photo."

"Well, who did?" demanded Jake. "The only other people who knew about those pictures were you and Aftab, and Aftab had to do his paper round after school, so unless. . ." He stopped. "Brendan, are you saying . . ?"

"Yes. I did it."

"But . . ." Jake seemed unable to grasp what he'd just been told. ". . . Why?"

"Because I disapprove of using cheap, degrading, tasteless photographs of half-naked women to sell newspapers." Brendan looked up, flushed and angry. "I know it sounds prudish and old-fashioned, but it's the truth." He hesitated, surprised by the vigour of his own outburst, before going on. "Anyway, when it became clear that you and Mojo were planning to include a Page Three girl in the *Post*, I decided something had to be done. I didn't think I'd be able to talk you out of it, so . . ."

Jake's face was registering total incredulity. "So you told Cormack and Jordan."

"Oh no!" At this point Brendan allowed himself a moment of quiet pride. "No, I did everything myself. I just called Mrs Mogridge's office from the pay phone outside the staff room, slipped into the darkroom when you'd gone, took one of the pictures, typed a note and . . . well, you know the rest."

Dave Anderson, who had begun to smile several seconds earlier, was now chuckling. "Brendan, you dark horse. You mean you . . . you stole one of their dirty pictures . . . and then . . . and then you . . ." He tried to finish the sentence but couldn't, suddenly doubling up instead with helpless, silent mirth.

"Hang on a minute," interjected Mojo. "There's something I don't get here. Brendan – you committed the perfect crime – you got away with it – so how come you didn't keep your mouth shut? Why the big confession now?"

Brendan linked the fingers of both hands and sighed.

"Guilty conscience, I'm afraid," he replied. "These last few days I've . . . well, what I did was wrong and two wrongs don't make a right." He looked across the room at Dave, who had just about regained control of himself. "Besides, it seemed unfair that Dave – or Charlotte and Lindsey come to that – should take the blame for something they didn't do. So you see I'm not remotely sorry for what I did, but I am sorry about the way I did it. I should have tried to persuade you – not taken matters into my own hands." Calmly and with great dignity Brendan got to his feet. "I apologize."

There was a brief, stunned silence during which Jake and Mojo exchanged a helpless glance. Then Dave turned round, leaned both hands on Jake's desk and tried unsuccessfully not to smirk. "Talking of apologies . . ." he began.

"Brendan! I mean, Brendan!" Mojo smacked his forehead with an open palm. "I can't get over it." It was twenty-five past twelve and he was standing outside a secondhand bookshop in the Portobello Road. Beside him Jake was riffling through a cardboard box full of Spiderman comics. Getting no response to his observation, Mojo squinted up at the cold, leaden sky and huffed a great cloud of dismay. " 'Course you know what this means you'll have to do."

"Yes."

"You'll have to apologize to Cormack as well."

"Yes."

"I mean, you called her a liar, Jake. In the student caff. In front of witnesses and everything."

Jake straightened up and fixed Mojo with a basilisk stare. "Thanks for the reminder," he said through gritted teeth.

They weaved their way through the noisy, bustling lunchtime crowds for almost fifty yards past window after window crammed with the ex-contents of Victorian attics before Mojo spoke again. "You think all this is my fault, don't you?" he began. " 'Cos you never really wanted to have a Page Three girl in the first place." He put a hand on Jake's shoulder to stop him. "It's true, isn't it?"

Jake turned stiffly, nearly knocking over an Indian woman laden with four carrier bags. "Look, let's just forget about it," he said with strained calmness. Then, as if more explanation was needed, "If you must know I've got other things on my mind."

Mojo removed his hand and they walked on towards Notting Hill Gate in silence for a while. "I still reckon it's censorship, though," he finally blurted out.

"Well, there's nothing we can do now, is there? It's over." Jake chopped the air with finality. "A dead issue."

"Yeah, I s'pose," agreed Mojo as they crossed the road. "Apart from you having to apologize to Cormack, that is." He turned up his collar, adding in a much quieter voice, "And apart from the blazing row I had with Lindsey just now."

"What row?" Jake stopped again, looking suddenly suspicious.

"While you were still talking to Dave. She came up to me in the common room and started gloating – you know, about Desirée."

"And?"

"And . . . well, I couldn't help it, *honest* . . . she was getting up my nose."

Jake had the feeling he was about to hear some very unwelcome news. "Mo, just tell me what happened," he said, stepping back into the doorway of a café.

"Well . . . like I say, she was all smug and superior, really winding me up, so I gave her a mouthful about how the *Post* would still be better than the *Gazette* whatever happened and she said 'Oh yeah?' and I said 'Yeah' and she said 'Well, why don't we settle this once and for all.

We'll each print 200 copies and flog 'em in the school on December 4th. That way we'll *really* find out which paper's best.' "

Jake blinked twice and pushed a band of wet hair out of his eyes. "So what did you say?"

"I said 'You're on'."

"Just like that."

"Mmm." Mojo was staring at the damp uppers of his Timberland shoes. He frowned. "But that's not the worst part."

"So tell me the worst part."

"Well, Hammond was there too, right? – and he thought it was a *great* idea 'cos it would give us a chance to find out about marketing and publicity and all that – you know, make the whole project more realistic."

"So it's official."

"Yeah. You're angry, aren't you? – I can tell." Mojo dug both hands into his pockets and looked up uncertainly, but to his amazement Jake was grinning from ear to ear. "You're *not* angry?"

"No, I think it's a brilliant idea."

"Really?"

"Yeah. Lindsey's right – this way we really will find out who's best. Don't you see? – they've blown it. They'll never be able to sell as many copies as us." His brow wrinkled. "The only thing is the printing, though. How are we going to . . ." He clicked his fingers. "I've got it – Pop Press! Of course!"

"Pop Press?"

"They're this printing company in Kilburn – Mum's using them for her exhibition catalogue. Apparently they're really cheap – in fact, if we gave them an ad in the *Post* they might even do the whole thing for free. That way, any money we made would be clear profit."

"Yeah!" Mojo's face lit up. "Make some cash *and* show Cormack and Jordan who's boss. What could be better than that, eh?"

Jake chuckled and glanced up. It had started to rain quite hard. "I tell you one thing . . ."

"What's that?"

"A sandwich." He jerked his head towards the café behind them. "What do you reckon?"

"Have we got time?"

"Yeah – it's only twenty-five to one."

Mojo nodded. "Come on, then."

Inside the sandwich bar it was hot and crowded. At first there were no free tables, but then Jake suddenly saw a couple by the window getting up. He pressed a pound coin into Mojo's hand. "Get us a cheese and tomato," he said, and made for the vacant seats. Alone for a minute he rubbed a clear porthole in the steamy window and peered at the buses, taxis, cars and windswept pedestrians outside. When Mojo arrived with a tray in both hands and two packets of crisps between his teeth he was still gazing out, but with a glazed expression which had more to do with thinking than looking.

"So what are all these 'other things' on your mind?" mumbled Mojo, noticing the glazed expression as he lowered first the tray, then himself, into position.

Jake turned. "Sorry?"

"A few minutes ago you said you had other stuff on your mind besides Desirée. Like what?"

Jake took a large mouthful of cheese and tomato sandwich. "Like my Mum," he replied, chewing pensively.

"What about her?"

"She's getting married again."

"Never! Who to?"

"This bloke I told you about – Graham." Jake put down the sandwich and slowly removed a piece of crust from one side. "Well, I say 'married' – she hasn't actually agreed yet, but he asked her the other night and she seems pretty keen. She's asked me to 'think it over'."

Mojo pulled open one of the crisp packets without taking his eyes off Jake's face. "Blimey!"

"Exactly." Jake pushed his damp cowlick back with the fingers of both hands. "I mean I've got nothing against the guy. He seems perfectly OK, and he and Mum obviously get on really well, and all that. It's just . . ."

"You don't want him to marry her."

Jake nodded reflectively as if the thought had just hit him. "Yeah."

"Well," Mojo sat back. "Hardly surprising, is it? I mean your Dad only died, what? – eighteen months ago?"

"Sixteen. Last July." Jake shrugged hopelessly. "Oh, I dunno. Everything seems confused at the moment. I can't get it all straight in my head. See, on one hand I want Mum to be happy – of course I do – but on the other I want things to carry on like they are. Daft, eh?" There was a pause, but Mojo didn't fill it. He just continued eating and waited for Jake to go on, which he did. "It's like . . . while she and I are together – just the two of us – well, life's pretty shambolic and it's tough going money-wise and all that, but it feels like Dad's still around in some weird way. He's not, but he is." Jake looked up. "Does any of this make sense?"

Mojo pointed to his full mouth, chewed for a few seconds and swallowed. " 'Course," he answered. "And you don't want some outsider coming in and taking his place. Makes total sense." He wiped his mouth with a paper napkin. "So what are you going to tell your Mum?"

Jake looked out of the window again. "To go ahead, of course. What else can I say?" He deepened his voice. "Mum, I want you to ditch your boyfriend. This relationship must stop!"

"No, but . . ."

Jake laughed and made an "Oh, well" gesture with his shoulders. "Just a matter of me getting used to it – that's all." He turned back to the table. "Anyway, what was it you were you going to tell me about Alex?"

"Alex?"

"Yeah – she gave you a lead on a big story or something."

"Oh, right. God – I'd completely forgotten, what with Brendan and Lindsey and everything." Mojo rummaged in his briefcase, finally producing a notepad which he dumped on the table. "Here we go." He flicked backwards and forwards through the pages, then suddenly stopped and looked up. "OK. This is the story. Are you sitting comfortably?"

Jake took another mouthful of sandwich. "Just get on with it," he mumbled.

"Right. Well, last Friday night Alex's brother Paul and two of his mates were walking down the All Saints Road at one in the morning when suddenly a police van rolled up and all these coppers piled out – about six of them."

"Yeah."

"Well, Paul and his mates started explaining they were coming home from a party and they hadn't done anything, but the coppers didn't want to know. They did all the names and addresses bit and searched them, then apparently the one in charge started getting really obnoxious – calling them names and pushing them around."

Jake frowned. "So what happened?"

"OK, eventually Paul said 'Look, enough's enough, right? Leave us alone.' Then the copper who'd been doing all the talking hit him."

"*Hit* him?"

"Yeah." Mojo looked up from his notes and met Jake's eyes. "Punched him in the face. After that they all got back in the van and drove off."

Jake didn't speak or move for a second, then he asked very quietly, "Are you sure about all this?"

Mojo nodded soberly. "It's exactly what Alex told

me. See, she knows we're putting a paper together and reckons we should talk to her brother." The door opened and a gust of cold air momentarily stirred one corner of the tablecloth.

"But why us?" asked Jake uncertainly. "Why doesn't he go . . .?"

"To the police?" suggested Mojo. "How can he?"

"No, I was going to say why doesn't he take his story to the real papers, the local press."

Mojo wrinkled his nose dismissively. "It's too small for them. 'Black teenager claims assault by police.' It would end up as three lines somewhere – if that."

Jake cradled the sugar bowl in one hand and spooned its contents abstractedly with the other. "Does Alex's brother know the name of the bloke who hit him? Did he get the number of the van? Anything like that?"

"He didn't get the number," Mojo replied, "but he reckons the one who hit him was called Dowson or Downey or something like that. Hang on," he flicked through his notes again. "Downing – that's it. And there's a description, too." He paused tensely. "What do you think? Should we go for it?"

Jake stroked his chin. "Can't say till we know a bit more, can we? – but I reckon a chat with Alex's brother can't do any harm."

Mojo smiled with relief. "I'll set it up then."

"Yeah." Jake straightened the tablecloth with both hands. "You set it up."

When Jake got home that evening there was a note waiting for him on the hall table. "G got last minute concert tickets. Back late. Chops in the fridge. M." Crumpling the note gently in one hand, Jake dropped his bag and walked through into the kitchen. Then, leaving the rock-hard chops to thaw, he bounded upstairs to his room and put on a U2 album at full volume. Kicking off his shoes he flopped onto the bed and lay there for a while, apparently content just listening to Bono's voice and staring at the ceiling. After the first side, though, he got up abruptly, turned the record over and padded across the hall to his mother's studio. The door was open. Very slowly he walked in, cleared a space on the paint-spattered floor and sat down. All around there were piles of stacked canvases, sketches, postcards from the Uffizi, the Louvre, the Prado, the Hermitage and the National, bottles of turpentine, brushes of all sizes, pieces of crumpled newspapers, rags, half-squeezed tubes of ochre, sienna, cobalt and magenta. Jake closed his eyes and let their collective smell stir up childhood memories for a few seconds before leaning back on both elbows with his eyes still firmly shut. He stayed in that position for nearly ten minutes, then realized with a sudden jolt that the record had finished. Shaking himself alert he clambered to his feet and stretched. What time was it? Ten to six. A portrait of his father stared out from a corner of the room. Jake stared back. "What's going on, Dad?" he asked it. "Just what the hell is going on?" Then, with only a brief detour to switch off the record player, he went downstairs and began cooking.

There was a portable black-and-white television in the kitchen, and once Jake had put the still half-frozen chops under the grill, he leaned to his left and turned it on. The news. Standing hands on hips for a moment he watched a burning car in a Belfast sidestreet, then turned away and began laying the table. Five minutes later the sound of the TV had become nothing more than a background drone to Jake's own thought processes. As he busied himself cutting bread, making a salad and looking for the mustard jar, it gradually slipped out of his consciousness until he was hardly aware of its presence in the room. Then, kneeling to get some peas out of the freezer, he happened to glance up and felt his mouth drop open. There, being led down the steps of a courthouse, through a jostling pack of reporters and towards a waiting car was

Antony Cormack. Quickly Jake turned up the volume.

". . . remanded on bail and scheduled to appear in court next Tuesday morning. Sir Patrick Mandelson, the chairman of Mr Cormack's company, Mercantile Finance, said he had no comment to make at the present time, but that this morning's arrest of Mr Cormack on insider trading charges related to the planned takeover of Strelson International came as a complete surprise. Now, from Bow St magistrate's court, it's back to the studio."

Chapter 7

Grimacing with concentration Mojo slid up to the twelfth fret. Then, with Jake playing a repeat chord sequence in the background, he held the note while his face became a mask of angelic calm. It didn't last, though. Half-opening one eye after a second he squinted across the rehearsal room to where Lauren was sitting, deep in thought about everything that had happened in the two days since Antony Cormack's arrest.

"Uh – ready when you are, Miss McGill."

"What? Oh, shit – did I miss it again?"

Mojo sighed and let his hand slide down the fretboard. "Lauren, what's wrong with you today? Come on – that's the third time in the last—"

"OK, OK," Jake broke in. "Let's just go back to the beginning." Mojo fell silent as Lauren rearranged her sheet music.

"Sorry, guys," she mumbled, clearly embarrassed. "Really. I'm sorry."

"Don't worry about it," said Jake. The rearranging stopped. "Ready?"

"Yeah."

"Ready, Mo?"

Mojo stared gloomily at the tuning keys on his bass and nodded.

"All right – from the top. And . . ."

When the rehearsal ended twenty minutes later, Mojo packed up quickly. "Right, I'm off," he announced curtly at the door. "Got some computer studies homework to finish for this afternoon. See you both later, eh?" – and with that he left, watched by a rueful Lauren.

"He's mad at me, isn't he?" she asked, as the sound of Mojo's footsteps disappeared down the corridor.

Jake made a mezza-mezza gesture with the flat of one hand and smiled. "He'll get over it." There was a brief silence, then Jake got up, closed the door and leaned against it. "Look," he began diplomatically, "I know it's none of my business, but . . . well, it's obvious this thing with Charlie's Dad is on your mind, right? Bound to be." Lauren carried on putting away her saxophone. "Anyway, I just wanted to let you know I realize what's going on, that's all, and . . ." he rolled his eyes and ground to a halt, folding his arms shyly. "Shut up, Jake."

"No, no," Lauren looked up. "It's OK." She ran one hand across the blue, crushed-velvet lining of her saxophone case. "Really – it's OK." There was a moment's hesitation. "But listen – tell me something."

"What?"

"You and Mo – I've been meaning to ask – are you guys going to write about Antony and the trial and everything in the *Post*?"

Jake walked back to the piano and sat down. "Well . . ." he scratched one side of his neck ". . . I'll admit we were tempted at first, but we had a talk yesterday and . . ."

"And?"

"And . . . we agreed not to."

Lauren beamed. "Do you mean it?"

Jake lifted his shoulders. "Yeah – well, we reckoned what with the whole *Post/Gazette* rivalry thing some people might say it was dirty tactics. Besides – take all the fun out of winning if we had an unfair advantage, wouldn't it?" He played a few random notes, then glanced sideways and chuckled.

Lauren smiled back, relieved. "Well, I guess that's one less problem for Charlie to worry about." She sighed. "This whole thing's hit her pretty hard, you know."

"Yeah – must have." Jake took a breath. "Come to that it can't be much fun for you either, stuck in the middle of it all." Lauren picked at a fleck of mud on her jeans. She had a sudden, powerful impulse to tell Jake *exactly* how much fun it was for her – to tell him about the row she'd overheard between Gudrun and Antony, about how upset Charlie really was, about Kyle still being in hospital, about nearly phoning her parents the night before to say she wanted to go home.

"Oh, I'm sure it'll all turn out OK," she eventually said, a wan smile on her face.

Jake nodded supportively and doodled a few more notes. "Talking of Charlie . . ." He cleared his throat and changed position slightly ". . . I, uh, I've been meaning to talk to her about something – something 'delicate', but I haven't had a chance in the last few days. You know how it is – she's always *with* people – so I was wondering . . ."

Lauren looked at him, glad to be distracted from her own thoughts. "Excuse me interrupting," she said, "but is this 'something delicate' what happened in the canteen the other day?"

Jake lowered his eyes and drew a circle on the piano stool's rough moquette covering. "Yeah," he confessed.

"Aha. I see. And you need a discreet venue where you can talk to her about it, right?"

"Right."

"Hmmmmmm." Lauren pondered. "Well, she's working at home with Lindsey this afternoon, but I think I know where you can talk to her alone tomorrow lunchtime. How's that?"

"Hi. Where are you off to?" It was 12.40 the next day and Mojo was chatting to Angela Mogridge in school reception as Jake went past with an intent expression on his face. "For a walk," he replied without stopping.

"Want company?"

"No, thanks."

Mojo turned back to Angela, who took off her glasses and peered after Jake's disappearing figure. "That young man has something on his mind if you ask me," she said.

Mojo scratched his chin, meditating. "I think you're right there, Mrs M," he agreed with a puzzled frown.

Outside Portobello Jake caught a bus. Flopping onto the nearest seat he paid his fare to a monumentally bored West Indian conductor then removed a small book from his back pocket. Whenever life began to feel out of control Jake always took refuge in his diary. Somehow, mentally planning the future calmed him down – made him feel more as though he was in charge of events and not the other way round. Oblivious to Kensington Church Street passing by outside in brilliant November sunshine he looked at the week ahead. OK, today was Wednesday. Tomorrow he had to see this bloke Paul, Alex's brother, about the police harassment story. Then on Friday there was a Nexus rehearsal. Saturday – here Jake muttered something to himself – was Kay and Graham's engagement party; then on Sunday the weekly Green Man gig. After that it was only ten days before 200 copies of the *Post* had to be ready. *Ten days!* Not long. Not long at all. And on top of all that . . . He looked up as the bus shuddered to a halt outside Holland Park. Well, this was it.

Walking up to the park gates thirty seconds later Jake suddenly stopped dead in his tracks and for a long moment seemed to be held back by an invisible force-field. Finally though he set his jaw and moved on again. No, it had to be done.

She was sitting exactly where Lauren had predicted, on a bench opposite the peacock enclosure. Dressed in a Jasper Conran coat and cream-coloured beret, she was shielding her eyes with one hand and holding a book in the other, while in front of her a thin stream of mothers with toddlers and solitary walkers passed by. Jake checked his step and took a deep breath. "OK, just do it", he told himself.

"Hi! What a coincidence!"

Charlie looked up at the figure striding breezily towards her. "Oh." Pause. "It's you." Pause. "Hello."

"Mind if I sit down? I was just, you know . . . passing, and I saw you." Charlie didn't reply but Jake sat down anyway. "Good book?" She showed him the cover. *Crime and Punishment* by Dostoyevsky. "Aahhh!" Jake nodded slowly. "Never read it."

"You should," Charlie replied, frowning. Or was she just squinting into the sunshine? Jake crossed his legs and looked away. Suddenly he didn't know what to say.

"Actually," he began, watching the only peacock in sight drag its massive tail along the grass like a folded fan. "Actually it's not a coincidence, meeting you like this. Lauren told me I'd find you here."

"Did she?" Charlie sounded less than pleased with the information.

"Yeah, she did. See, I wanted to talk to you about what happened the other day – you know, in the student caff when I . . . when I called you a liar." Jake coughed into his right hand. "I wanted to apologize."

Charlie slowly closed her book and examined Jake's face for signs of sincerity. He was still watching the solitary peacock trailing towards a weeping willow, but as he became aware that she was looking at him, he turned round. "I really am sorry," he said. "I was wrong. It wasn't you – it was Brendan. I know that now, and if it's any consolation I feel a complete prat about the whole thing."

A tiny flicker of pleasure played momentarily around the edges of Charlie's mouth, but she repressed it instantly. "Thanks," she said. "Now, if you don't mind . . ." She lifted Dostoevsky into view, indicating that she'd like to be left in peace to carry on reading.

"Right." Jake stood up then immediately sat down

103

again and folded his arms. "There's something else," he resumed.

"What?"

"I saw about your Dad on the news the other night." There was an ominous silence from the other end of the bench which Jake ignored. "And I thought . . . well, two things, really. First off, Mojo and I decided not to do anything about it in the *Post*."

"I know. Lauren told me." Long pause. "I'm grateful."

"And then I thought . . . I dunno . . . maybe you'd like to talk about it or something."

"Talk about it?"

"Yeah." Jake lifted one shoe onto the bench and began tying its lace, which had come undone. "See, I know it's not the same, but I remember when my old man first got ill, I didn't talk to anybody about it – not even my Mum. I mean not properly. It wasn't that I didn't want to, I just didn't, that's all. Seemed easier at the time – but looking back I think it made things even worse than they really were. Made me feel more . . ." he let go of the re-tied lace, ". . . alone." Absorbed in memories of his father Jake barely heard the very quiet "Yes," but when he looked at Charlie's face there were two damp streaks running down her cheeks. Almost angrily she pulled a tissue out of her pocket and swiped at the tears with a series of quick gestures while Jake watched. "Look – shall we go for a bit of a walk?" he suggested. "Get a cup of tea at the Commonwealth Institute or something?" Charlie peered down at the cover of her book for a long moment, then nodded briefly. "Right then," Jake went on, standing up. "Come on."

A coach party of old-age pensioners had just arrived, so the Commonwealth Institute self-service cafeteria was busy.

"It all seemed so unreal," Charlie began, once she and Jake had installed themselves at a corner table. "I mean

Lauren and I just had this phone call at school on Monday, and when we got home there were all these people – reporters – outside the house. Two policemen had to help us through, and then when we got in, my mother was standing in the kitchen and she looked . . . somehow she looked so . . ." Charlie opened the fingers of both hands ". . . vulnerable. And I said 'What's going on? What's all this about?' and she said, 'Sit down – something's happened.' You see *she'd* only heard the news about an hour earlier. Sir Patrick, that's my father's boss, phoned her after Dad was arrested – before they released him on bail, I mean." Charlie cleared her throat and pushed a strand of hair behind one ear. "Anyway, that's how I found out."

Jake stirred his tea. "OK, let me get this straight. What your Dad's actually supposed to have done is tip off some people in the City? Is that it? He told them about this Strelson takeover thing so they could buy shares before the price went up."

Charlie nodded. "Basically, yes – only of course he didn't."

"So he reckons he's innocent," said Jake.

"He doesn't 'reckon' anything." Charlie's eyes flashed angry, unconditional certainty across the table. "He *is* innocent."

"OK. OK." Jake made a truce gesture with both hands. "I didn't say he wasn't." There was a short silence. "But what about the £2 million all the papers are on about? How did it get into this bank account in the Bahamas, and how come all the cheques had his signature on them?"

Charlie frowned at the sugar bowl as if it was a faulty crystal ball. "He doesn't know," she replied quietly. "But it isn't *his* account like the press have been saying – it's the company's account. He's just one of several people who have access to it for temporary loans and financing projects – things like that. It wasn't him that put the money

105

in – that's the point. Somebody was forging his signature – covering their tracks so that if the whole thing ever got out, Dad would be held responsible."

"But he doesn't know who it was?"

"No – at least, not yet."

"Ah." Jake took a mouthful of tea and didn't reply. Charlie watched him warily.

"I know what you're thinking," she went on. "How can she be so sure? Well, I know my father – that's how. He told me he didn't do anything illegal and I believe him, so that's all there is to it, OK?"

Jake gave her a small supportive smile. "OK." He put down his cup. "I *am* on your side, you know."

Charlie stopped looking unconvinced and leaned back, lacing her fingers in her lap. "Sorry," she murmured. "It's just – well, maybe I'm not used to you being nice, that's all." She half-smiled. "I mean, what with the *Gazette* and the *Post* and everything we always seem to have been at each other's throats up to now."

Jake crossed his ankles and shrugged. "Yeah, well."

"Yeah, well," mimicked Charlie with the same shrug. For a moment they just smiled at each other across the table, then simultaneously became aware of an elderly couple hovering a few feet away. The man was doggedly clutching a loaded tray while the woman gazed helplessly around looking for somewhere to sit. Collecting their coats, Jake and Charlie got up.

"Oh, thank you," said the woman with a polite smile. "So kind. But please don't hurry away on our account."

"No – that's all right. We've finished," said Jake.

The woman laid a hand on his arm. "Well, if you're sure, dear." She lowered her voice to a significant whisper and nodded towards her husband. "You know a long time ago *we* were young and in love – just like you two." She beamed at Charlie. "Hard to believe, isn't it?"

Outside, a colourful row of international flags fluttered thirty feet above Jake and Charlie's heads as they emerged into dazzling sunshine a few moments later. "If only they knew, eh?" Charlie said, leading the way to the bus stop. Jake glanced across and took in her profile, the cream beret, her hair dishevelled by the breeze. He hesitated for a second, then laughed weakly.

"Yeah," he agreed. "If only they knew."

A look of total bafflement crossed Mojo's face as he looked out of the common room window. Jake and Cormack? Walking back into school together? Smiling?

"Brendan – do you want another card or not? Hurry up – the bell's going to go in a minute."

"Ummmmm – yes."

"Right." Dave twisted a card off the top of the pack. The Queen of Hearts. Pursing his lips enigmatically Brendan picked it up and added ten more matches to the pile on the centre of the table. Mojo exchanged a rapid glance with Aftab. "Do you reckon he's bluffing?"

"Perhaps I am, perhaps I'm not," chipped in Brendan, neatening the already perfect fan of cards in his hand and smiling sweetly. "You'll just have to wait and see, won't you?"

"Yes, Brendan, I suppose I jolly well will," replied Dave, doing an exaggerated imitation both of Brendan's prim tones and his smile.

Across the room Lauren and Lindsey broke away from a group at another table and came over. "You're just in time to see me do some serious winning in the all-important final of 'The Portobello Lunchtime Poker Club' play-offs," muttered Mojo as the girls arrived.

"Hmmmm, quite possibly," replied Lindsey, casting a glance at Mojo's hand. "After all, with a royal flush you should be home and dry, shouldn't you?" Mojo, Dave,

Aftab and Brendan all looked at each other, then at Lindsey, who had arranged herself on a plastic-covered bench next to Lauren and begun leafing through a photo-romance magazine. "Did I say something wrong?" she enquired, placing one hand over her mouth like a guilty little girl. At this point Lauren started to get the giggles and within a few seconds was propped against Lindsey, her shoulders shaking uncontrollably.

"Your faces," she finally managed to say, pointing wavily at the poker players.

"Oh yes, very droll," muttered Mojo, throwing his cards onto the table. "Very amusing."

Dave looked up at the clock on the wall. "Well, that's that. Not worth dealing again – it's five to one. Come on, Brendan, let's go and get a cup of coffee."

Mojo leaned his chair back on two legs and sighed heavily as Brendan and Dave walked away. "Lindsey, you are such a pain in the ass sometimes – has anyone ever told you that?"

"Oh come on," Lindsey riposted, trying to keep a straight face. "Can't you take a joke?" Judging by his expression, Mojo couldn't.

"That wasn't a joke – that was nothing like a joke – that was just . . ." he searched for a satisfactory adjective and found one ". . . puerile!"

"What?!" exclaimed Lindsey. "*Puerile?* Look who's talking!" She crossed her legs and raised a very judge-mental eyebrow. "Coming from someone whose idea of fun is looking at photographs of women's chests, I think that's a bit rich."

Mojo sucked in his cheeks and nodded slowly. "Well at least I don't read kids' comics," he responded acidly.

"Here we go," muttered Aftab.

Lindsey closed the photo-romance magazine she was holding and turned to face Mojo directly. "This is not a kids' comic," she said, waving the publication in question at him. "It's a perfectly respectable magazine. At least it

108

deals with real life and . . . and . . . and relationships!"

"What?" Mojo threw his head back and cackled. "That crap isn't about relationships – it's about second-rate Mills and Boon fantasies, that's all." He drew an invisible thought bubble above his own head and looked up at it, biting his bottom lip and simpering "I wonder if Wayne feels the same way as me".

"All right, all right," interrupted Lauren, looking at Mojo and putting a restraining hand on Lindsey's arm. "Let's not get— "

"That is *so* patronising," Lindsey carried on regardless, her angular face registering a mixture of disdain and outrage.

"No it's not," replied Mojo pleasantly. "I'm just pointing out that photo-romance sells a fantasy just as much as Page Three pictures, only instead of sex the fantasy is all that, all that . . ." he waved a dismissive hand at Lindsey's magazine, ". . . happy ending, lovey-dovey bullshit."

Lindsey's eyes narrowed. "And what's wrong with wanting a happy ending?" she asked murderously.

"Nothing – but it's not how the real world works!" Mojo turned to Aftab for moral support. "Am I right or am I right?" Aftab shrugged, unable to disagree.

"See?" Mojo indicated his mute supporter as evidence and sat back, resting his case.

"Well maybe, just *maybe* there's more than one way of looking at 'the real world'," hissed Lindsey, getting to her feet.

Mojo stood up too and brought his face very close to hers. "I imagine we'll find out on December 4th," he replied through clenched teeth. Meanwhile at chair level Aftab and Lauren exchanged pained glances and both shook their heads. Then the bell went.

Jake gazed wearily around the empty Tube compartment rattling and crashing its way between East Acton and

White City. Adverts for temp agencies, a crumpled newspaper, sweet-wrappers, a manic lager can rolling between the seats. He sighed and went back to the notebook on his lap, flicking randomly through its pages and hearing Paul Leary's voice again as he did so.

"We were just walking home – that's all we were doing."

"After he smacked me in the mouth I looked down and there was blood everywhere."

"Downing – that's what one of them called him."

"Oh yeah, I'd seen him before, all right. He's a sergeant at the Pembridge cop shop."

As the train pulled into Notting Hill Gate Jake closed the book and stuffed it into his overcoat pocket. Then he stood up, waited for the doors to roll open and stepped onto the platform. For a moment he just stood there, apparently lost in thought, oblivious to the doors rolling shut behind him. "Damn it," he said aloud. "Damn it, damn it, *damn* it." Then, as a great gust of hot, stale air rushed through from a westbound train he slowly shook his head and set off towards the escalator.

It was half past nine by the time Jake finally got home. "Hello," said Kay's voice from upstairs as he shucked off his coat and walked through into the kitchen.

"Hi."

"How was the band rehearsal?"

"It wasn't a rehearsal," Jake called back, munching a biscuit and leafing absently through a copy of *Homes and Gardens*. "I had to go and see somebody. It's this newspaper thing I'm doing for school."

"Ahhh," Kay replied. Then, a few moments later. "Oh, that reminds me, Maurice phoned about an hour ago. Said could you call him back when you got in." Jake let the thick, glossy magazine slap shut and reached for another biscuit.

"All right. Thanks."

"Have you eaten?"

"No, but don't worry – I'll do an omelette or something."

"Could you? I'm up to my eyes."

Twenty minutes later Jake left the frying pan to soak and returned Mojo's call. "Hello, Mr Johnson, it's Jake Shepherd. Is Mojo there, please?" He could hear the distant thudding rhythm of a rap record in the background. "Just one minute, Jake, I'll call him," replied Charles Johnson. The thudding continued for a few moments, then stopped abruptly. Soon afterwards Mojo came on the line.

"Hi. So how'd it go?"

"Well, you were right," Jake began, hauling himself onto a kitchen stool. "God, Mo, I've never seen anything like it. I mean the guy's face is a mess. He could hardly talk and it's a week since it happened. A week!"

"Did you speak to his mates as well? The ones who were there when it happened?"

"Yeah."

"And they backed him up?"

"Yeah."

Mojo gave a low-key whoop of triumph. "Sounds like we've got ourselves a front page story. Listen – I'll get onto Carlton tomorrow about taking a photo."

"Mo . . ."

"He was a bit pissed off about the Desirée thing, but I'm sure when he knows what an important . . ."

"Mo, we can't put it on the front page."

Mojo stopped. "What do you mean we can't put it on the front page?"

"Because . . ." Jake began winding the telephone cord around one finger ". . . because there's a problem."

"What problem?"

"I can't talk about it now. I'll tell you at school tomorrow."

Mojo paused suspiciously. "This hasn't got anything

111

to do with that cosy little chat you and Cormack had yesterday, has it?"

"Don't be daft. How could it?"

"I don't know, but . . . well, I don't understand. You just said . . ."

"I know what I just said." Jake looked at the kitchen ceiling despairingly. "The story's there and it's important, but I don't think we can put it on the front page, that's all. Not just an accusation – not without cut and dried proof."

"What do you *want*?" This time there was real anger in Mojo's voice. "The guy was beaten up, he's got witnesses, he was left bleeding on the ground!" Jake didn't reply. "I thought you were the one who wanted to do investigative journalism. Well, this is *it*, Jake – it's the best story we've got by miles and now you're telling me you don't want to put it on the front page?"

Jake got up and pushed the kitchen door shut. "Look, will you calm down. I'm not saying it shouldn't be in the *Post* . . ."

"Oh no, you're perfectly willing to put it in the *Post* – as long as it's stuck away on an inside page. Great. Terrific. Well, if that's the way you feel about racial harassment maybe it's time you got yourself a new co-editor."

"Mo, for God's sake, I've said I'll explain tomo . . ." But it was too late – Mojo had hung up. Jake stared at the buzzing receiver in his hand for several seconds then suddenly banged it down and went to do the washing up.

Ten minutes later he made himself a cup of coffee and trudged upstairs, retrieving his overcoat from the hall floor en route.

"Hello," said Kay, looking up from some paperwork as he walked into her studio. He gave a small wave by way of reply and leaned against a wall, his coat hanging off one shoulder. "What you doing?" he asked.

"Paying bills. My favourite occupation."

112

Jake made a little circle in the air with his forefinger. "Whooppee."

"I know."

They both chuckled, then Jake yawned, pulled up the blue armchair and sat down. "Is that who's coming on Saturday?"

"What?" Kay followed his eyes to a sheet of paper pinned on the cork noticeboard above her desk. "Yes. There's only going to be about twenty, though. It's a drinks do really – not a party at all."

"Right." Jake removed a non-existent hair from the arm of his shirt.

"Just Graham's family and a few of his closest friends, and the same on our . . . side." Kay paused, seeing something she couldn't quite read in Jake's face. "You haven't changed your mind about us having a party have you? I mean, I know you agreed when I first suggested it, but you seem— "

"No, it's fine." Jake straightened his position in the chair. "Really. I think it's a great idea. I'm just a bit tired, that's all." He yawned again. "You know – long day. In fact— " Getting up, he walked across to his mother and kissed her on the forehead. "I think it's time for beddy-byes."

She held on to his wrist as he turned away. "Jake?" He looked down at her face.

"What?"

"I just wanted . . . well . . . I just wanted to say how much it means to me, you accepting things the way you have."

Jake shrugged. "What's to accept? Graham's a nice guy – that's all that matters, isn't it?" They looked at each other and Kay smiled. "Yes."

"Night, then."

She squeezed his hand for a moment longer before releasing it. "Goodnight."

Jake crossed the landing, went into his own room and closed the door. Then he took out his notebook and flicked through until he found the quote he was looking for.

"Oh yeah, I'd seen him before, all right. He's a sergeant at the Pembridge cop shop."

"And who's Graham Paxton?" Jake murmured, throwing the notebook onto a chair. "Chief Inspector Graham Paxton? My stepfather-to-be?" He walked over to the bed and sat on it despondently. "The officer in charge of Pembridge police station – that's who."

Chapter 8

"I've just remembered something!" Lindsey exclaimed, snapping her fingers and smiling delightedly. It was Sunday afternoon and she was lying on the Cormacks' living-room carpet surrounded by sheets of paper and photographs.

"What?" asked Charlie from the sofa.

"That portrait of Jake Shepherd you told me about weeks ago," Lindsey explained, "the one his mother was painting – we were going to put a photo of it in the *Gazette*, weren't we?"

"Yes, I know, but that was just a . . ."

"Charlie, we have *got* to do it." Lindsey screwed up her face in a momentary paroxysm of exquisite anticipation.

"Why?"

"Don't you see? We could put it on page 3 and run a whole spoof thing about 'Gorgeous, pouting, nubile sixteen-year-old Jake Shepherd' – you know, really turn the tables on all that sexist bilge they ogle every . . ."

"I don't think so," Charlie interrupted, flicking through the folder on her lap. "It would just be petty."

Lindsey frowned and placed both hands firmly on her hips. "But it was your idea in the first place."

Charlie carried on flicking and didn't look up. "Not to do what you just said. Anyway, I've changed my mind, OK?"

"Why?" Lindsey narrowed her eyes slightly. "You're not going soft on the opposition, are you?"

"No."

"Why then?"

This time Charlie raised her eyes. "Well, for one thing

we've already got enough stuff to fill the *Gazette* twice over. And for another . . ." she sighed ". . . look, we're supposed to be producing a newspaper with *integrity*, Lin – that's the whole point, isn't it?" She paused, for emphasis rather than reply. "A serious paper – a positive paper. If we did what you're suggesting we'd just be sinking to their level. That's all I'm saying."

"Hmmm." One side of Lindsey's mouth turned up uncertainly. "I suppose so." The agreement was grudging and followed by a dramatic exhalation. "I still think it's a brilliant idea, though."

"What about these?" Charlie held up two photos taken at the previous summer's Notting Hill Carnival. Each showed a policeman dancing with black revellers. "Which one shall we use for the race relations article?"

"The one on the left," said Lindsey, after a second's scrutiny. She placed a pencil against the cleft in her chin. "You don't think we could put it on the front page, do you?"

Charlie looked at the photo again. "Well . . . I still reckon the drug rehabilitation picture's better. Where is it?" She looked through the pile of photos beside her and pulled out the one she was looking for. "Don't you think?" It showed six unsmiling teenagers standing outside a ramshackle house. Over the door was a sign saying "The Ladbroke Centre".

Lindsey took the picture and examined it more closely. "It's a big grim."

"Not 'grim' – strong," said Charlie. "That's why it's so good. Every one of those kids has come off drugs thanks to the Ladbroke, and half of them used to be at Portobello. It's relevant, Lin."

Lindsey chewed the end of her pencil. "They all look so miserable, though. I mean, I know it's an important subject, and I know their advertising money's paying half our printing costs but surely the front page should have something more . . ." She stopped as the telephone on the smoked-glass coffee table rang and Charlie leaned forwards to answer it.

"Hello?" Pause. "I'm afraid he's out." Sigh. "I'm his daughter – look, who is this?" Longer pause. "No, I have absolutely nothing to say – nothing at all." She put the phone down abruptly and looked at it with disgust.

Lindsey watched her. "Is that what it's like?"

Charlie swallowed and nodded. "Happens three or four times a day." Neither of the girls spoke for a moment, then Charlie cleared her throat and turned back to the *Gazette*. "Anyway, what were we talking about?"

"How do you *cope*?" asked Lindsey, refusing to change the subject. "I mean, wouldn't it just be easier to take the phone off the hook or something?"

Charlie shook her head. "That wouldn't work. Dad still needs to talk to his lawyers, and he's got friends calling all the time . . ." she smiled ". . . in fact most people have been really kind – you know, asking how they can help, wishing him luck – things like that. It's just these stupid tabloid reporters that go on and on. One of them rang at half-past midnight yesterday – can you believe it?"

Lindsey's expression indicated that she couldn't. "It must be awful," she murmured – then, lifting up a pile of photos and typewritten pages, "Weird, isn't it? I mean us doing this while your father . . . you know."

Charlie leaned back against the sofa and hugged both knees. "Weird isn't the word," she said. " 'Surreal' more like. But I tell you one thing – the *Gazette* means more to me now than ever."

Lindsey nodded. "I can see how it would." She smiled. "Let's get on with it then. Have you got the agenda?"

"Ahh – I think so – somewhere." Charlie lifted two folders and retrieved a sheet of paper. "Yes, here it is." She pushed a lock of hair behind one ear. "OK, we've gone through the race relations piece, the drug thing, your interview with Mr Busby about the future of Portobello, my piece on local job schemes . . . what else? – oh yes,

117

we talked about advertising, typesetting, printing, finance, blah, blah, blah, bah, *blah* . . ." she ran a finger down the list and looked up, smiling. "So all that's left is arranging a publicity slogan and sorting out the launch."

"Well, I've had a few ideas about publicity," Lindsey began. "What do you think of this?" She spread her hands in the air to indicate a banner headline. " 'The *Portobello Gazette* – At last – a "good news" paper'."

"I like it!"

"Honestly?"

"Yes, it's terrific. We could . . ." The phone rang and both girls froze.

"Don't answer it," said Lindsey in an urgent whisper.

Charlie hesitated briefly, then picked up the receiver. "Hello?" she asked tentatively. There was a moment of silent tension, after which she visibly relaxed. "Oh, hi. What? Half past seven? OK – I'll tell her. No, she's out in the garden. See you then." Pause. "Yes, I will. 'Bye."

Replacing the phone she smiled at Lindsey, who had one hand to her throat. "Your father?"

Charlie smiled. "Yes."

At four o'clock the two girls had finished their meeting and were just packing up when the door opened and Lauren walked in. She was wearing a long, rainbow-coloured scarf and carrying her saxophone case. "Hi guys," she said and sank gratefully into an armchair. "God, I'm exhausted."

"How was it?" asked Charlie. Lauren gave her a thumbs-up-sign. "Great. Tremendous audience – treeeeeemendous. Best yet. We played really well, too." She beamed. "And . . ."

"And?" asked Lindsey.

"*And* . . ." Lauren hesitated, holding up two pre-empting palms. "Look, I know you two aren't exactly fans of my co-band-members but, well it's no good, I've got to tell you anyhow." She unwrapped her scarf and leaned forward, cheeks red, eyes shining. "After we finished

118

the set, this guy came up, said he really liked the music and could he talk to us. Then he took out this card and gave it to Jake."

"So who was he?" asked Lindsey, trying not to look too intrigued.

"His name's Phillips – Drew Phillips," Lauren continued. "And-I-think-he-wants-to-manage-us. Can you *stand* it!" She mugged a silent scream at the ceiling.

"He wants to manage Nexus?" repeated Charlie unnecessarily.

Lauren reined in her enthusiasm for a moment. "Well, first he says we need to make some demos, then he's going to set up a meeting with us after Christmas, but he seems really enthusiastic." The beam returned.

"That's amazing," murmured Lindsey. "God, how exciting." She chuckled. "I mean even if Jake and Mojo *are* in the band, it's still exciting."

"It certainly is," echoed Charlie.

"Anyway," Lindsey looked at her watch. "Exciting or not, I must dash. I've got a judo lesson at four thirty."

Lauren blinked. "I didn't know you took judo lessons."

"Oh yeah." Lindsey was busy collecting her things together. She stood up and smiled. "It's fun – you should come along sometime." She turned to Charlie. "Right. There's nothing else we have to talk about, is there – *Gazette*-wise, I mean?"

"I don't think so," replied Charlie. "A few details about the launch maybe, but we can talk about them at school tomorrow." Lindsey moved towards the door. "Don't bother seeing me out. 'Bye, Lauren."

" 'Bye."

" 'Bye, Charlie."

" 'Bye."

As the front door shut, Lauren looked across the room at Charlie. "Judo?"

"Mmm – she's been doing it for a couple of years,

apparently. Got a green belt and everything."

Lauren whistled. "Impressivo!"

Charlie tucked her legs onto the sofa and smiled. "So's your Mr Phillips. Do you think he's serious?"

"Looks that way. Oh God, I can't buh*lieve* it!" Lauren pulled both ends of her scarf tight with her fists. "I mean I can't believe how different I feel right now from this time yesterday, and all it took was one phone call from Kyle and then this guy coming up after the gig."

Charlie laughed. "No more talk about going home, then? – now that Kyle's definitely going to be 100% OK, I mean."

Lauren shook her head. "I guess not . . ." she paused ". . . unless things here . . . you know . . ."

"Oh don't worry about that. In a few weeks everything round here will be back to normal."

"You really think so?"

"Of course." Charlie flicked back her hair and smiled with all the confidence she could muster. "Bound to be."

Under a pewter-coloured sky Jake and Mojo strode purposefully towards the cricket pavilion. "All right, all right, maybe I was a bit hasty the other night," Mojo admitted. "But I didn't know about your Mum's boyfriend— "

"Fiancé."

" 'Fiancé' then, did I? All I knew was you didn't want to put our best story where it belonged – on the front page."

Jake held out the palm of one hand. "I thought we went through all this yesterday after the gig," he began. "*I* should have told you about Graham straight off the other night, *you* shouldn't have flown off the handle, blah-di-blah-di-blah – let's not go over the whole thing again, OK? What we've got to do now is deal with it."

By this time they had reached the pavilion, a run-down, peeling, white clapboard shed on the edge of the cricket pitch. As Mojo fumbled in his pocket for the key, Jake jogged on the spot in an unsuccessful attempt to keep warm.

"Hurry up," he pleaded. "It's freezing out here."

"Moan, moan, moan," replied Mojo, turning the key and pushing open the reluctant door with one shoulder.

The inside of the pavilion was surprisingly comfortable, with four fold-away wooden chairs, a small table, two faded, tattered oriental rugs on the floor, some leatherbound books on a shelf and even a sink in one corner. Next to the sink were a handful of teabags and a kettle. Jake headed straight for these while Mojo organized the single-bar electric fire bracketed to one of the walls. Five minutes later they were fully installed, the pavilion was warm and two mugs of tea were steaming on the table.

"Are you sure Vic Drake didn't mind you borrowing the key for this place?" asked Jake, pulling some papers out of his briefcase.

"'Course," replied Mojo, grinning. He jerked a thumb towards the leatherbound volumes on the bookshelf. "I told him we wanted to look up the cricket team's results last year – you know, background for a sports article. He lapped it up."

Jake chuckled. "You've got a devious streak a mile wide, you have."

"Me!" Mojo pretended to look put out. "Watch who you're calling names, sonny." He folded his arms. "Anyway, whose idea was it to come down here in the first place? – 'away from prying eyes'. At least I'm not paranoid."

Now it was Jake's turn to look offended. "I am not paranoid! All I said was I didn't want Lindsey and Dave and Brendan and everybody else snooping around while we're sorting out this Downing thing."

Mojo smiled smugly. "Yeah, well I've got news for

you – that's called being paranoid." He took a slurp of tea, then glanced at Jake's unsmiling face over the rim of his cup. "Uh-oh – sense of humour failure."

Jake looked at him. "We have actually got a problem here, in case you hadn't noticed."

Mojo blinked. "Well I had . . . *actually*. But it's not the end of the world. We can still have a laugh, can't we?" Jake considered this for a long moment, then rubbed his eyes, straightened up and nodded.

Twenty minutes later the pavilion looked like a very small library after a whirlwind. The entire floor was covered with pieces of paper, photographs and page plans. Parking a pencil behind one ear, Mojo consulted the notepad in his hand. "Right – let's go over this one more time. We're making Paul Leary's story the lead on 2, but *not* mentioning Downing by name."

Jake looked up from his own notes. "Yeah. And you're sure you don't mind – about it not being on the front page?"

"I said, didn't I?"

"Yeah, but . . ."

"Jake, it's OK." Mojo fiddled with an elastic band. "I mean, you're right, we can't prove Downing did it, and you'd be in deep shit with this Graham guy if he didn't. I can see all that. I'm not happy about it, but I can see it."

Jake ran the fingers of both hands through his hair. "I'm not happy either, but we're doing the right thing. OK, go on."

"Meanwhile the staff-cuts article moves to the front page, my truancy piece runs on three with the review section, sport, soap up-dates, etc, etc and four –" he riffled through his notes "– four, four, four, *four* . . . is the alcohol abuse feature, the strip cartoon, a vox pop on 'What would you do if you won £1,000,000?', the horoscopes and the gossip column." Jake got up and moved to a long, glass window overlooking the cricket pitch. Outside, flurries of sleety rain were driving across the sodden grass. "Which brings us to the question of log books," Mojo went on.

"Hmmmm?"

"Log books." Mojo helpfully waved a black folder in the air. "Remember? These things? We're supposed to keep a record of who does what?"

"Oh yeah," Jake shivered slightly, still watching the weather, then turned round. "Right," he said. "Log books it is, then."

It was five to one when Jake and Mojo left the pavilion. "And you reckon these Pop Press people will print up 200 copies for nothing if we give them a free half-page ad?" asked Mojo, turning up his collar.

"Yep," replied Jake, locking the door. "That's what they said on the phone, anyway. Apparently they do fanzines and stuff like that all the time, so they reckon a bit of publicity in a school paper would make it worth their while. Anyway, I said I'd go round to their place in Kilburn tomorrow night to talk it over." He put the key in his pocket as Mojo frowned.

"I thought that was supposed to be tonight."

"Can't tonight," replied Jake as they set off, heads bowed against the elements, towards the main school building. "I'm going to the theatre."

"Wooooohhh!" Mojo's voice went into a spasm of sarcasm.

"Bog off."

"All right, all right. What are you going to see?"

Jake scowled up at the sky. *"Hamlet."*

"Who're you going with?"

"Guess."

"Mum and her fiasco?"

"In one."

Mojo turned round and started walking backwards. " 'Cos just for a minute I wondered if it might have been old Cormack." The eyebrows jiggled. Jake looked at him and carried on walking.

Mojo decided to try another topic of conversation. "So listen, what are we going to do about putting some demos together for our friend Mr Drew Phillips? I mean I don't see how we'll have any *time* before the Christmas holidays what with the *Post* and everything."

Jake grunted in agreement. "Yeah – I was thinking the same thing last night. That'll be OK, though. We break up on the 14th, right? – well, all we need is a couple of days in the studio and then we can get the tape to him."

"Right. Fine. Just like that." Mojo squinted sideways at Jake, his hair flattened by the wind. "Studios aren't exactly free, Jake. I mean we're talking major spondooliks here. £200 – £300, maybe."

Jake replied with a small, knowing smile. "I've been thinking about that, too, and I reckon I've got the answer – well, maybe."

"Yeah?"

"Yeah. See when Dad died he left this trust fund – separate from all the life insurance stuff Mum got. The idea was for me to get some money when I left school."

"So you're going to leave school?"

"No, birdbrain – shut up and listen. I'm going to ask Mum if I can have an advance – just enough for the demos."

Mojo turned round and began walking backwards again, his briefcase slung over one shoulder. "Do you reckon she'll let you?"

"Who knows? Worth a try, though. What've we got to lose?"

Mojo spread his one available palm in a carefree gesture. "Exactly. What've we got to lose? Only a once-in-a-lifetime chance of megastardom, that's all." He shrugged nonchalantly. "Who wants to be rich and famous, anyway?"

As the house lights went up, a tide of applause roared and surged round the Olivier Theatre. From her seat in the dress circle Kay Shepherd glanced round the auditorium, then turned to Jake. "How long's the interval?"

Jake consulted his programme. "Uh – twenty minutes."

"Come on, then," said a voice on the other side of Kay. "Let's go and get a drink."

Outside, the lobbies were crammed with knots of theatre-goers. Positioning himself next to a tall, sand-filled ashtray Jake settled to watch them while Graham and Kay went to the bar. A tall, elegantly-coiffed woman in shimmering gunmetal-coloured silk walked haughtily past. Two Japanese businessmen burst into laughter. A small, bored-looking girl swung idly from one side to the other holding a brass stair-rail with both hands behind her back. Jake watched them all and let the buzz of "crowd speak" wash over him. Then a minute later he looked across the room and in the same objective way caught sight of his future stepfather striding across the lobby. Chief Inspector Graham Paxton. Forty-five, square-jawed, tall, well-built, going a bit thin on top. Piece by piece Jake put together an identikit picture. What else? Serious, dependable, an Arsenal supporter, a classical music fan, considerate, quiet . . . in fact, all in all a thoroughly nice bloke. "It's true," Jake murmured under his breath, "he *is* a thoroughly nice bloke," then a thought came to him – quickly, insistently and without any shadow of doubt attached to it. "I wish they'd never met."

"Right – here we are – half of lager, wasn't it?"

Jake took the extended glass and smiled. "Thanks."

"So, what do you think?"

For a second Jake looked nonplussed. "Oh, the play" – he took a mouthful of lager – "Great!"

"You're doing it for A level – isn't that what your Mum told me?"

125

"Yeah, that's right."

Graham undid the middle button of his suit jacket and chuckled. "A levels. You know when I did them they'd only just started – a bit like GCSEs today." He sipped his orange juice and raised a "that reminds me" finger. "By the way, what about this newspaper project of yours – how's that coming along?"

Jake made a tiny involuntary noise in the back of his throat. "Well, it's . . . uh . . ."

"God, what a scrum!" said Kay, emerging from the group of people behind them. "It's like the January sales in there." She smoothed her dress in a mock-elegant gesture and smiled, first at Graham, then at Jake. "Anyway, we're here to celebrate, so I'd better stop complaining, hadn't I?"

Graham slipped an arm round her shoulder. "Yes, we *are* here to celebrate," he said, lifting his glass up. "So let's do just that. Happy birthday, darling, and here's to the future." Jake watched as Graham and his mother briefly kissed. For a moment afterwards they beamed at each other then both turned towards him.

"Oh, right," he agreed and took a mouthful of lager. "Happy birthday, Mum."

During the second half of the play Jake's concentration kept coming and going. Ophelia strewing flowers round the stage, Gertrude lifting the poisoned goblet to her lips, Hamlet duelling with Laertes, then dying in Horatio's arms – they all swam in and out of his own thoughts and became confused with other images – Paul Leary's face, Charlie Cormack's cream-coloured beret, Drew Phillips holding out his business card in the back room of the Green Man. There was something else, too – another layer which had nothing to do with either of the others – a layer of, what was it? – well, instincts and feelings, really. Nothing he could put his finger on, just hopes and anxieties all jumbled up together. Caught up in

126

this three-way current of impressions Jake lost all track of time and was amazed when all the actors in the play were suddenly lined up across the stage bowing to a crescendo of noise. Was it over then? He glanced at his watch then at Kay applauding beside him. Yes, it was over.

Afterwards, walking across Hungerford Bridge to where Graham's car was parked, Jake wanted to join in the conversation. Somehow, though, he couldn't – it was as if something was stopping him. "You're very quiet," Kay finally said, as a train on the railway bridge beside them clattered past into Charing Cross station.

"Still lost in the play, aren't you, old son?" remarked Graham with a smile.

Jake looked at him. "Yeah – that's it," he replied, hauling himself into the present and returning the smile. He cleared his throat. It was time to make an effort. "Thanks for buying the tickets, by the way."

"My pleasure," said Graham. Kay watched her son fondly for a moment, then turned towards the river. "Will you just look at that view," she sighed, moving to a niche in the bridge and leaning both hands on its stone parapet. Jake and Graham both stopped as well, one on either side of her, to admire the view. In front of them the whole of the South Bank and the Embankment were lit up and reflected in the Thames, while St Paul's and the City, dominated by the Nat West Tower, glittered and sparkled in the distance.

Nobody spoke for a moment, then Graham took a deep breath of night air and said, "Well, I suppose now's as good a time as any." He paused. "There's something I've been meaning to tell you both."

Kay turned, curiosity in her eyes. "Oh?"

"It's not definite yet," Graham went on, "but it's something I want you to think about."

Kay laughed. "Well, we can't think about it until we know what 'it' is, can we?" Jake watched Graham's hand fiddling with a coat button. What was going on?

"All right – well, it's this. I've been asked to take on a new job. I haven't accepted yet, and it wouldn't happen for three months anyway, but it would mean a big promotion and a lot more money." Another pause. "It's not here, though – it's in Cornwall." He looked first at Jake, then at Kay. "Now I know we'd planned to stay in London, but if you think about it, moving out makes a lot of sense. We could afford a bigger place, a higher standard of living – get away from all the stress and pressure of living in London . . ." by now his face had become eager with explanation ". . . don't you see? – it would be a completely fresh start."

Kay turned back towards the river and didn't speak for several seconds. "Cornwall," she finally repeated in a distant voice, her eyes fixed on the dark, fast-flowing water.

"So Friday's the big day, huh? You guys ready?" Lauren opened her saxophone case and looked across the rehearsal room.

Mojo licked both palms, smoothed back the hair at his temples and grinned. "You'd better believe it," he said.

Lauren chuckled. "Just checking." She carried on putting her saxophone away, then paused, head to one side. "Mo?"

"Hmmm." He was bent over the fretboard of his bass trying out a new riff.

"You and Jake aren't going to do anything . . . silly . . . are you?"

Mojo stopped playing and looked up. "Silly? How do you mean?"

"Well, you're not going to pull any stunts on Friday to make sure the *Post* does better than the *Gazette*, are you?" After a moment Lauren's voice resumed on a new, pleading note. "See, I'm thinking about Charlie. She's upset enough as things are, with the preliminary hearing coming up next week."

Mojo blinked four times in rapid, disbelieving succession. "Are you saying we should deliberately let Cormack and . . . and . . . and . . ."

"Her name's Lindsey."

". . . sell more copies than us just because of *that*?"

"Noooo." Lauren gently fastened the clasps on her saxophone case and sat on the floor. "I just don't want any trouble, that's all." She smiled ruefully. "In fact, I don't see why you're having this whole 'who can sell the most?' thing, period, as you well know."

Mojo looked at the tuning keys on his guitar. "Healthy sense of competition, I suppose. Nothing wrong with that, is there?"

Lauren decided not to reply. Instead, folding her legs into a half-lotus position she allowed a few seconds to pass, then changed the subject. "So – uh – when's Jake going to ask his Mom about this money for the demo studio?"

Mojo stopped playing and scratched his chin thoughtfully. "Well, he said he was going to do it the other night when they went out for her birthday, but apparently he never got round to it."

"Ahhh." Lauren nodded.

"In fact," Mojo went on, "ever since that evening he's been acting a bit weird – really quiet and fed up. Like today – saying he wasn't in the mood to rehearse. Weird."

"Yeah, I wondered about that," Lauren agreed. "Jake's normally so easygoing." She frowned. "You don't think maybe he did ask his Mom and she said 'no'? Maybe that's it – maybe he just doesn't want to tell us."

Mojo looked unconvinced. "No, I reckon it's something else." But before he could voice any opinion about what that "something else" might be, the bell went.

Lauren groaned. "Already?"

Mojo checked his watch. "Yeah – it's quarter past one." He got to his feet. "Come on, it's Media Studies now, isn't it?"

Lauren pressed a forefinger into each cheek and gave a 1950's TV commercial grin. "Sure is!"

Walking down the corridor they continued their conversation about demo recordings. "Because if Jake *can't* get the money," said Lauren, "I could always try my folks – put the squeeze on them for a loan, I mean. How about yours – do you think they'd help out?"

Mojo chuckled softly to himself. "Well, let's just say I wouldn't hold my breath if I was you."

Lauren looked mystified. "You wouldn't hold your breath? What does that mean?"

Mojo translated. "It means 'No way, José'."

"Oh, right." Lauren rolled her eyes. "God, I thought I already spoke English."

When they got to Room 28, Charlie, Dave, Brendan and Aftab were already there. "Oh yes," Brendan was saying as they walked in, "I think it's quite possible there won't be any teachers before long."

Thinking of the *Post*'s front-page story, Mojo came to a sudden halt. "You what?"

Brendan looked up. "Oh, hello, Maurice – Charlotte and I were just discussing the possible expansion of computer teaching – Aftab and I have written an article on it in *Millenium*."

"Oh!" Mojo exhaled with relief. "Fine."

"Yes, it's all rather interesting. From our research it seems likely that by the year 2000 some parents will be legally entitled to withdraw their children from schools and educate them from home by computer. After that – well, it would be logical to assume that the number of teachers will gradually decline until there are none left at all – just 'educational computer programmers'. Interesting possibility, don't you think?"

Mojo frowned earnestly. "Extremely," he agreed. Then, pausing only to straighten Brendan's tie, he sauntered over to where Dave was sitting and flopped into a vacant seat.

"Ah – just the man I wanted to see!" Dave began, looking up from his copy of the NME. "I've got a proposition for you."

On the other side of the room, Charlie had finished her conversation with Brendan and was leaning against Lauren's desk at the back of the room. "So how was your rehearsal?" she asked, examining her nails.

"Good," replied Lauren, "except Jake wasn't there."

"Oh?"

"Mmm. Said he 'wasn't in the mood'." Lauren paused, rolling up the sleeves of her sweater. "Charlie, *you* don't know what's been wrong with Jake recently, do you? He seems awfully . . . what's the word . . . subdued."

Charlie stopped examining her nails and examined Lauren instead. "Why should I know?"

"Oh, no reason. It's just that . . . well, you said you guys had a chat in Holland Park the other day and I wondered if . . ."

"Well, whatever you wondered, the answer's 'no'." Charlie went back to her nails. "And stop looking at me like that."

"Like what?"

"You know perfectly well."

"No, I don't."

"Yes, you do."

Genuinely confused, Lauren frowned for a second, then shrugged and began unpacking her schoolbag.

"I – uh – I talked to Mr Busby just now, by the way," Charlie went on lowering her voice. "You know, about the hearing and everything. He says it's OK for me to take time off. He was really sweet about it."

Lauren smiled. "Great."

131

"He said you could have time off, too, if you wanted." The two girls looked at each other.

"Well, I . . ." Lauren seemed taken aback. "I hadn't thought about it. I mean I *had*, but it's a family thing and I assumed you and your Mom would just . . ." she trailed off into silence as Charlie looked straight into her eyes.

"Lauren, I'd like you to be there."

"You would?"

"Yes. I've got a feeling I'm going to need all the moral support I can get." Charlie swallowed hard. "I mean I know Mum and the lawyers and everyone will be around, but . . . will you come?"

There was a brief silence before Lauren replied, and when she did her voice quavered slightly with uncertainty and emotion. "OK," she said. "If that's what you want."

"Why, good afternoon, Ms Jordan – and how are *you* today? Heard any 'good news' lately?"

Lindsey, who had just walked through the door, answered Mojo's question with a curt "Drop dead, creep", and strode past him to the back of the room, where, having sat down, she started slamming books onto her desk. "God, it is going to give me such satisfaction to see that sexist little twerp put in his place on Friday," she muttered grimly to Lauren and Charlie.

"What was that?" enquired Mojo, craning forwards, one hand to his right ear. "Didn't quite catch it over here."

At that moment Jake arrived and Mojo's attention immediately switched away from goading Lindsey. "Jake! Jake! Come here! Quick!" Jake ambled over, exchanging a barely noticeable moment of eye contact with Charlie as he did so.

"What's up? he asked, lowering himself into a chair as Mojo and Dave both leaned forward eagerly.

Mojo grinned at Dave. "Tell him," he prompted.

"Well," Dave cleared his throat in a businesslike manner, "I'm in charge of the entertainment committee for the Christmas Party, right? – and I was wondering if Ne . . ."

"Good afternoon, everybody. Sorry I'm late, but you can blame the head for calling yet another lunchtime staff meeting. Now . . ." Phil Hammond closed the door behind him as conversation around the room sputtered to a halt. "I know this doesn't affect everybody, but before we start I want to have a quick word about Friday – just to check we're all clear on what's happening. Could I have your attention please, Maurice, since you're one of the people this applies to? Thank you. It's one stall each in the school foyer, 20p per copy, stock of 200 copies per title, publicity posters *nowhere* except on the noticeboard and selling only between 12.30 and 1.15 on the day itself. Understood?"

There was a mumbled chorus of more or less positive responses from Jake, Mojo, Lindsey and Charlie.

"Fine." Phil leaned back and exhaled, smiling with satisfaction. "Well, then, all that remains is for me to wish both the *Portobello Post* and the *Portobello Gazette* good luck, and may the best publication win."

Lindsey gave Mojo a glacial stare, then half-turned and launched a dazzling smile at Phil. "Oh, don't worry, sir," she purred. "I'm sure it will."

Chapter 9

Kay Shepherd's pink 2CV stood in a Kilburn side-street outside Pop Press Printers. Flakes of snow had just begun to whirl out of a pitch-black sky and form a thin layer on its roof, but inside Kay was oblivious to this change in the weather. She had the heater full on, her eyes were shut, and she was gently swaying from side to side in time with a Nina Simone cassette. Suddenly a loud rapping noise at the window shattered her reverie. At first Kay didn't seem to realize what was happening, then she peered out, smiled, and reached over one shoulder to open the back door. "Strewth-o-riley," mumbled Jake, clambering in and simultaneously blowing on his blue and white fingers. "OK – pass them over, Mo." In the rear-view mirror, Kay watched as an enormous pile of newspapers held by two disembodied arms was transferred to Jake. The owner of the arms then climbed in, took half the papers back from Jake, slammed the door and grinned triumphantly.

"Everything OK?" Kay asked the mirror.

"Yeah, fine, Mrs Shepherd," Mojo replied.

"Here, have a look," said Jake, passing a copy through from the back seat. "I think they've done a really nice job."

Kay switched on the car's inside light. "Hmmmm, very smart. Who did the layout, them or you?"

"Us," said Mojo, exchanging a proud glance with Jake. "We did everything except the typesetting and the printing. Design, layout, paste-up, everything!" He removed the top copy from the pile in his lap and gazed at it in mute admiration.

"This front-page story," Kay went on. " 'WHO'S FOR

134

THE CHOP? – six to go in spring staff cuts.' How did you find out about that?"

Jake stopped blowing into his cupped hands. "Sorry, Mum, we journalists aren't allowed to divulge our sources." Kay adjusted the rear-view mirror until she had a clear view of Jake's face. "Well, we're *not*," Jake emphasized, seeing her sceptical expression.

Mojo leaned forwards and spoke in a stage whisper. "Let's just say we've got our methods, Mrs Shepherd."

"Oh, come on," said Kay. "Is it really true? – The school's going to get rid of six teachers?"

"Yep," Jake confirmed, not flippant any more. "See what happened was we got hold of an internal report that says Portobello's really up the creek financially and they've got to cut back on staff, otherwise the whole place might have to close."

"But that's awful!" Kay turned round as a sudden thought occurred to her. "Just a minute – you're not going to get into trouble for printing this, are you? I mean, surely that report must have been confidential?"

Jake shrugged. "They can't deny the story's true."

"Oh Jake, are you sure? Shouldn't you . . .?"

"Mum, it's a *scandal*! Staffing levels at Portobello are bad enough as it is – we can't afford to lose six teachers. All we're doing is telling the kids about it early. They've got a right to know – it's going to affect their education."

"Yes, but . . ." Kay seemed uneasy. "Does Mr Hammond know you're putting this on the front page?"

Jake and Mojo exchanged another glance. "Not exactly," said Mojo. "But he's not supposed to have editorial control, anyway."

"No," Jake confirmed. "And besides, the staff cuts piece is good investigative journalism – he can't object to that, can he?"

"Hmmmm." Kay still sounded unconvinced. "What about Charlotte Cormack and her friend – are they printing the story?"

135

Mojo snorted derisively. "Hardly – and if they did the headline would probably be 'LOTS OF JOBS TO REMAIN AFTER OVERSTAFFING PROBLEM RESOLVED'. He chuckled delightedly, grabbing Jake's arm, ". . . or . . . or . . . how about 'EARLY RETIREMENT MOVE WELCOMED BY GRATEFUL TEACHERS'."

Laughing, Jake punched him in the shoulder – "Prat!" – after which Mojo hit him in the arm and they both started laughing even harder. Leaving them to it with a benign shake of the head, Kay turned to pages two and three of the *Post*. There, the photograph of Paul Leary's bruised and swollen face immediately caught her eye and she was just about to read the story when Jake tapped her on the shoulder. "We'd better get a move on," he said, still laughing and fending off Mojo at the same time.

"Oh, right." Kay folded the paper. "Is it OK if I hang on to this by the way?" she asked. "I'd like to read it properly later on."

"Yeah, of course." Jake was obviously delighted. "Be our guest."

Ten minutes later the car pulled up outside a block of flats in Acton. "I really appreciate this, Mrs Shepherd," said Mojo, attempting to unwedge his knees from the back seat and pass Jake 100 copies of the *Post* at the same time.

"My pleasure," Kay replied. "Have a nice time with . . ."

"Alex."

"Alex. Are you going out?"

"No." Mojo checked he was out of rear-view mirror range, then gave Jake the eyebrow treatment. "We thought we'd just have a quiet evening in."

"I see." Kay nodded slowly. "Oh, Maurice," she turned round. "I nearly forgot. What time are we picking you up tomorrow?"

Mojo looked blank, his mind on other things, then

saw Jake sigh and point a vertical finger at the stack of newspapers on his lap. "Oh yeah – 'the big day'. Uh – is twenty to nine too late?"

"No, twenty to nine is fine," said Kay.

"Great." Mojo opened the back door and began extricating his lanky frame from the 2CV. "See you in the morning, then."

Once he'd gone, Jake transferred to the passenger seat. "You wouldn't *believe* the reaction this newspaper thing's getting at school," he said with evident satisfaction. "All the kids are talking about it – and did I show you the posters Mojo and I put up?"

"Mmmmm." Kay turned the ignition key. "Last week – remember?"

"Oh yeah." Jake fastened his seat belt and grinned sheepishly. "Sorry – got a lot on my mind."

"Ditto." Kay shot him a sympathetic look, indicated right and pulled out into the stream of traffic. "In fact before we go home do you mind if we pop up to Camden Town first? – I want to see about a few things in the gallery."

Jake shook his head. "No – that's fine. I'd quite like to see the place, actually."

"Really?"

"Yeah."

Kay brushed a wisp of hair off her forehead and moved up into fourth gear. "Then you shall."

When they arrived, the gallery owner was on the phone. "Mr Sternbach's talking to a client in New York," his secretary whispered, inching the office door shut behind her. She was tall, beanpole thin and had a sixties' beehive hairdo. "Would you like a glass of wine while you're waiting? We've got some in the fridge."

Two minutes later the secretary had retreated to her desk and Jake and Kay were strolling round the gallery's upper room, wine glasses in hand. "So this is it," said

Jake, backing off from a small abstract canvas entitled "Still Waters" by Polly Fowler and glancing round.

Kay took a mouthful of sweet German wine. "God I hate Liebfraumilch," she grimaced. "Yes, this is it. What do you think?"

"I like it."

"It's got a nice atmosphere, hasn't it?"

"Yeah – your stuff will look really good in here." Conversation stopped for a minute while mother and son each looked at various pictures. Then they sat down on a bench in the middle of the room and waited for Pierre Sternbach to finish his call to New York.

"So – uh – have you thought over what we talked about last night?" asked Jake, as casually as possible.

"The money for these tapes of yours?" Kay nodded. "Yes."

"Is that 'yes, you've thought about it' or 'yes, I can have it'?"

This time Kay smiled. "Both."

"Oh, Mum – that's terrific!" Jake reached over and hugged his mother, taking her completely by surprise so that she spilled some of her wine on the floor.

"Thanks. You won't regret it – I promise."

Kay shook her right hand dry and chuckled, head on one side. "Well, I'm sure it's what you Dad would have wanted." She looked at Jake tenderly and reached out to smooth his hair.

"Yeah," he agreed. "I think you're right." The gallery's calm white silence reasserted itself for several seconds, then Kay said: "As a matter of fact, there was something I wanted to ask *you*, too."

"Oh?"

"I wondered . . . well, I just wondered what you thought about this job offer Graham's had." Jake didn't reply. "Ahh." Kay slowly withdrew her hand. "It's like that, is it?"

"Like what?"

"You don't want to talk about it."

Jake shifted uneasily. "I didn't say that."

"Well, you haven't mentioned it since the other night at the theatre."

"Neither have you."

Kay smiled and adjusted a button on the cuff of her raincoat. "All right – so we've both been avoiding it. I'd still like to know what you think, though."

"All right." Jake took a deep breath. "I don't want to go."

"Why not?"

There was a long silence. "Because . . . well, all my friends are here for a start, and I've only been at Portobello for a few months, and I *like* living in London – I've never lived anywhere else, and . . ." he frowned at the unvarnished, pale wooden floor and sighed. "Look, what's the point of me going on like this? It's not really my decision. I mean, Graham obviously wants the job otherwise he wouldn't have said anything, would he? – and you're marrying him, so that's that – we're going."

Kay transferred her wine glass from one hand to the other. "Not necessarily."

A moment passed. "What do you mean?"

"Well," she ran her finger round the rim, "I've gone over and over it – from *everybody*'s point of view, and . . . frankly, I don't think it's a good idea, either."

Jake stared at his mother, a look of astonishment spreading across his face. "Really?"

"Hmmm."

"But what about Graham? I mean . . . have you told him?"

Kay shook her head. "No, not yet. I wanted to talk to you fir— "

"Kay, I'm terribly sorry to have kept you waiting." Jake swivelled round and saw a man dressed in an immaculate dove-grey suit walking briskly towards them. He was about fifty with an aquiline nose, sallow skin and large hooded eyes. A lemon-yellow handkerchief protruded from his top pocket. "New York!" he intoned, rolling his eyes and shuddering as he bent down to kiss Kay on the cheek.

"That's all right, Pierre," she replied.

"No, it is *not* all right – it was very rude of me," Pierre Sternbach retorted, "but as the client in question is *seriously* rich and *seriously* interested in buying over half of Polly's work . . ." he spread his arms in an elaborate "what could I do?" gesture, indicating the paintings on the wall. "Now!" – he turned his attention to Jake, "and who is this?"

"Oh, excuse me – Pierre, this is my son, Jake. Jake – Pierre Sternbach."

"Ah yes, of course – the portrait. I knew your face was familiar." Pierre extended his right hand. "Pleased to meet you."

Jake shook it. "Likewise." Then, as Pierre led Kay downstairs, he lingered a moment and drained his glass with a smile of private satisfaction. Well, that was good news. But even as he turned to leave the room, word association led him from "good news" to the *Portobello Gazette* and the smile quickly disappeared.

"Hi!" Lauren was standing self-consciously in front of Jake and Mojo's stall in the school foyer, peering down at several stacks of the *Post* on a trestle table.

"Hi," mumbled Jake, checking his watch. Twenty past twelve. Ten minutes to go. "OK, OK" he told himself – "the papers, the cash box, the publicity posters . . . was that everything?" Behind him, Dave and Aftab were laying out a large sheet with the message "TODAY'S NEWS FOR TODAY'S PEOPLE" blazoned across it in red paint, while on the other side of the foyer Lindsey, Charlie and Brendan were busy preparing the *Gazette*'s stall.

"What can I do for you?"

140

Lauren sighed. "This is so embarrassing. Lindsey asked me to come over here and buy a copy of the *Post* because basically she didn't want to do it herself." She made a "can you believe it?" face. "I mean, petty or what?"

Jake smiled understandingly. "Mo," he wiped his forehead and spoke to the floor.

"What?" it replied.

"Should we let Lauren buy a copy before half past do you think? It's for Lindsey."

First Mojo's head, then a hand holding a lump of Blu-Tack appeared above the table. "Yeah – why not?" he grinned. "They'll need *some*thing to read while they're not serving customers."

"Oh, very nice. Very constructive," replied Lauren, digging into the pocket of her dungarees. "What is it? 20p?"

"Yeah – that's right," said Jake, accepting the coin and examining it proudly. "Mo, look – our first income as newspaper tycoons."

"God, I'll be glad when this is over," muttered Lauren, turning away and trudging back across the foyer.

"Quick, quick, give it here," said Lindsey as soon as Lauren reached the *Gazette* stall. Grabbing the *Post* she eagerly scanned its front page, snorted derisively, turned to pages two and three, skimmed their contents – "Uh-huh, uh-huh, uh-huh – God, how predictable" – flicked to the back page, briefly perused that, too, and then turned the whole thing over again. "Just as I thought," she said, looking up with ill-disguised satisfaction. "Sensationalism, rumours, sloppy research, half-baked non-stories and cheap tabloid innuendo. Tacky, tacky, tacky."

She picked the paper up between thumb and forefinger and was about to consign it to a wastepaper basket when Lauren gasped: "But you haven't even *read* it."

Lindsey paused, still holding the *Post* suspended in mid-air like a pair of dirty socks above a laundry basket.

141

"I don't need to," she remarked conclusively, releasing her grip on the word "need".

"Lindsey, have you considered the possibility that you're being a tad judgemental here?" asked Lauren, rescuing the *Post* and dusting it off.

"Nope," replied Lindsey, and went back to unfurling a large banner. So far all that was visible of its message was

THE *PORTOBELLO GA*
AT LAST A GOOD NE

"Oh, brother," Lauren muttered to herself pulling up a chair and beginning to read.

"Is that what I think it is?" asked Charlie, returning from a trip to the art department in search of sticky tape.

"It certainly is," sneered Lindsey. "And every bit as rancid as we always knew it would be. Did you have any luck?"

"What?"

"Sticky tape."

"Oh – yes, here." Charlie passed over a roll of Sellotape and then bent over Lauren's shoulder. A few seconds later, hearing a throat being cleared, she looked up and saw Aftab standing in front of the *Gazette* stall.

"I was just wondering . . ." he remarked, but Lauren had already begun giggling.

"Don't tell me," she said. "You want to buy a copy of the *Gazette* for Mojo." Aftab nodded soberly, holding out a 20p coin. "Here." Charlie handed over a copy from the nearest stack, pushing away Aftab's proffered 20p as she did so. "Tell him there's no charge. We'll soon have more than enough money – we don't need his."

"Eh?" Aftab looked nonplussed.

"You heard," said Lindsey, then as Aftab walked away she turned to Charlie and murmured, "Nice touch."

"Thought you'd like it," Charlie replied.

Behind them, Brendan had now pulled up a chair next to Lauren. "Mmmm," he began, casting a nervous glance in Lindsey's direction before adding in a low whisper, "As a matter of fact this truancy article is rather good . . . well written I mean. So's the cover story."

Lauren nodded in agreement. "I know. The reviews, too. And look at this story about the guy who got beaten up by the police. God, the picture's gruesome, but what they've written is really powerful stuff." She turned to the back page. "I mean you've got to hand it to Jake and Mojo – I'll admit I didn't think they could actually do it, but they've put together quite a hard-hitting paper."

On the other side of the foyer Mojo was scribbling on a large sheet of cardboard with a felt-tip pen as Jake, Aftab and Dave carried out a parallel inspection of the *Gazette*.

"And look at this!" cackled Dave. "Blimey – would you credit it? As if a photo of Hammond and his sprog wasn't enough, the crawlers have actually interviewed *Busby*!"

"Yes indeed," Aftab read aloud, imitating the headmaster's Yorkshire accent. "There is a great deal for Portobello College to be proud of at the moment. We are strong, confident, and moving forward to a bright future."

"How can the moron *say* that?" Dave's mouth hung open in sheer disbelief. "Next term he's sacking 20% of the staff and here he is telling us how marvellous everything's going to be. What a hypocrite!" He looked at Jake, eager to have his opinions reinforced. "Isn't he, eh?" Jake took a deep breath and checked his watch yet again.

"Almost half past," he said, standing up.

"Hang on, hang on." Dave grabbed the sleeve of Jake's baseball jacket. He looked puzzled. "You haven't said a dicky bird while we've been looking at the *Gazette*. What's up?" Jake looked at him and was just about to reply when the 12.30 bell went, instantly followed by the sound of doors opening, raised voices and footsteps clattering down corridors.

"Nothing's up. I'm just a bit on edge, that's all," said Jake, freeing his sleeve. He turned towards the trestle table as Aftab prodded Dave in the shoulder.

"Come on, I'm starving."

"Oh right." Dave began walking towards the canteen with Aftab. "See you after lunch then," he shouted back to Jake and Mojo. "Good luck!"

Jake waved, then immediately turned to Mojo, who was making last-minute adjustments to the TODAY'S NEWS FOR TODAY'S PEOPLE banner.

"Mo, we've got problems," he hissed frantically, waving the *Gazette* in his face. "I mean, OK, there are a couple of naff things in here, but basically it's good – the paper quality's better than ours, the design's sharper and . . . and it makes the *Post* look . . . well . . . amateurish."

He scanned the *Gazette's* centre spread, gnawing his bottom lip anxiously, then looked up, expecting to see a similarly anxious Mojo. Instead, what he saw was a relaxed, smiling Mojo.

"Didn't you hear what I said?" he hissed, louder this time. "We've got problems – I reckon they're going to sell more than we are."

"No, they're not."

"They're not?"

"No." Mojo shot the cuffs of his sweatshirt and adjusted a bow tie he wasn't wearing. "Cos I just took care of it."

"How?" As Jake put his question a pair of double doors behind him burst open and a tide of Portobello students surged into the foyer.

"You know Hammond fixed the price of the papers at 20p."

"Yeah."

"Well, he didn't say we couldn't *cut* our price, did he?" With that, Mojo ducked out of sight, reappearing

144

a moment later with a large sheet of cardboard which he leaned carefully against the trestle table at an angle which hid it from the *Gazette* stall. Felt-tipped on this makeshift hoarding was the slogan "SPECIAL LOW PRICE. ONLY 18P."

"Mo!" exclaimed Jake, gratefully pumping his partner's hand as a noisy crowd of inquisitive customers began to form in front of the stall. "You are a genius – an utter and complete genius!"

"Good God! Shepherd! Johnson! Is this *true?*" Adrian Brand stood, transfixed, staring at Jake and Mojo over the front page of the *Post*. All round him Portobello students were calling out, laughing and pushing, but Adrian Brand hardly seemed to notice them.

"Sorry, sir?" replied Mojo, handing out change from a biscuit tin. "Oi! Oi! One at a time!"

"I said is this true?" Adrian Brand turned the front cover round so that Mojo could see it.

"Oh yeah," Mojo smiled disarmingly.

"But how could . . .? The head hasn't said a . . . Right. We'll see about this." And with that the music teacher spun on his heel, shouted "Make way" and forged an authoritative path through the jostling crowd.

Meanwhile Jake was manhandling another pile of newspapers onto the trestle table. "This is the last lot," he grunted, dropping them with a dull thud. "When these have gone, we've sold out. Brilliant, eh?" He turned to Mojo, who glanced up from the change tin, his forehead glistening with beads of sweat.

"Yeah. And that's not all," he grinned, jerking his head towards the other side of the foyer. "If you want the really good news, take a look over there."

"I don't understand it. I simply do not understand it," muttered Lindsey, her lips barely moving. Standing next to her a depressed-looking Charlie sighed.

145

"Me neither. How can they be doing so much better than us? It just doesn't make sense." She gloomily examined the small knot of customers drifting round the *Gazette* stall, comparing them unfavourably with the small sea of humanity packed round the *Post*'s trestle table, in the middle of which Jake and Mojo were intermittently visible.

"Oh, come on, there's still twenty minutes to go," replied Lauren, trying to sound chirpy. "And look on the bright side – you've sold over 50 copies."

Lindsey was clearly in no mood for bright sides. "Which means we've got 150 left," she replied tartly.

"But that's because you've produced a quality newspaper with longer articles and fewer photographs, not to mention an editorial approach which is unfamiliar to the market," Brendan chipped in, perched on a stool just behind Charlie. "And it's a well-known fact that the quality press never sells as many copies as the . . ." he groped for an adjective ". . . 'popular' papers. I mean it's only to be expected, surely?"

Charlie and Lindsey both turned round, looked at him, looked at each other and then turned round to face the front again.

"Come on Bren," said Lauren diplomatically. "I think it's time we went to see if there's any delicious grilled liver left in the canteen. Don't want to outstay our welcome, do we?"

Brendan peered at her uncomprehendingly, then Lauren drew a finger across her throat and the penny dropped. "Ah yes," he remarked, and picked up his briefcase. "Come to think of it I am rather hungry."

"So we'll – uh – see you guys in a few minutes, OK?" said Lauren. Receiving no answer she pushed Brendan gently in the back and together they walked off towards the canteen.

A few minutes later Phil Hammond hurried into the

146

foyer carrying a stack of exercise books. "Hi, how's it going?" he asked Charlie and Lindsey. "Sorry I wasn't here earlier, I had to mark this lot" – he indicated the stack of books. "Sold many?"

Charlie did her best to look positive. "Mmmm yes, quite a few, actually."

"Well, you're just about to sell another one," said Phil, rummaging in his jacket pocket. "Here." He handed over 20p, took a copy of the *Gazette* and was on the point of opening it when a loud chorus of groans went up on the far side of the foyer, quickly followed by two loud whoops of delight. Looking up from the *Gazette*, Phil smiled. "What do you think all that's about?" he asked.

"At a rough guess, I'd say they just sold out," replied Lindsey shortly as the top of Mojo's head became visible bouncing up and down behind the *Post* stall.

A moment later her theory was confirmed as Jake's voice boomed out over the complaints of fifty or sixty disappointed customers. "Sorry, folks – sold out. That's right – they've *all gone*. Well, you should have got here earlier, shouldn't you?"

Phil raised his eyebrows, then glanced sideways at the three untouched piles of *Gazettes* in front of Charlie and Lindsey.

"Please," Lindsey began, holding up both hands. "Just don't say anything understanding, OK? I don't think I could bear it." Having opened his mouth to do exactly that, Phil satisfied himself with breaking into a sympathetic grin.

"OK," he agreed. "I won't."

By ten past one the foyer was almost deserted. On one side Mojo and Jake were counting their takings while on the other Charlie and Lindsey were taking down the *Gazette* banner. Meanwhile Lauren, Brendan, Dave and Aftab had all drifted back after lunch and were helping to pick up discarded copies of the newspapers. In

147

the middle of the scene, Phil Hammond sat on an isolated chair absorbed in Charlie's article on drug rehabilitation. An unread copy of the *Post* lay folded on his lap.

"Thirty-four pounds, 20 pence," said Jake, dropping one last 20p coin into the biscuit tin with panache. "Not bad, eh partner?"

Mojo chuckled. "Not bad at all. In fact I'd say we've . . . uh – oh."

"What?" Jake looked up from the figures he'd been jotting down on a scrap of paper as Mojo nudged him sharply in the ribs.

"They're coming over."

Charlie and Lindsey were both walking across the foyer heading straight for them.

"So they are," agreed Jake. There wasn't time to say anything else.

"Afternoon, girls," Mojo began pleasantly as they stopped in front of the trestle table. "Sorry, but if it's copies of the *Post* you're after, I'm afraid they've all gone."

Charlie shook her head amiably, exercising a good deal of self-control. "No, we didn't come here for that," she replied. "We simply came to offer our congratulations."

"Eh?" Mojo shot a sideways glance at Jake and scratched his chin. "Do what?"

"Obviously the *Post* has sold out and the *Gazette* hasn't, so, since we're not bad losers, we thought it was only fair to come over and say 'well done'." At this point, Lindsey, who had been staring dejectedly at her shoes throughout Charlie's brief speech, suddenly noticed something. It was the corner of what looked like a sheet of cardboard and it was sticking out from under the TODAY'S NEWS FOR TODAY'S PEOPLE banner. With one foot she casually pulled it a few inches towards her, and, reading upside down, slowly made out the words SPECIAL LOW PRICE.

"Just a minute," she said quietly and stooped down

to examine the sheet of cardboard more closely. "What's this?"

Only then did Jake and Mojo realize, simultaneously, what she had found. Instantly the self-satisfied smirk left Mojo's face. "Oh that," he blustered. "That's just a . . . you know . . . a— "

"I can see what it is," said Lindsey, holding out the now fully-exposed SPECIAL LOW PRICE – ONLY 18P sign for Charlie to inspect. Her breathing began to accelerate. "Why, you slimy— "

"Now hold on, I can explain. See what you don't seem to— " But it was too late. Eyes blazing, Lindsey had already dropped the cardboard sign and marched around the table. Then, grabbing a handful of Mojo's jacket, she bent double, called out "Hyaaaa!!" and threw him a full 360° over her back in one swift movement that ended in a dull, resounding thud.

Hearing the noise, Phil Hammond looked up, as did Lauren, Aftab, Dave and Brendan.

"What was that?" asked Lauren.

"That," replied Lindsey, gazing down at the horizontal, groaning Mojo, "was revenge." Then, panting slightly and dusting off her hands with grim satisfaction, she stalked out of the foyer, almost bumping into Adrian Brand as she did so. He was coming in the opposite direction and looked almost as single-minded as she did. So single-minded in fact that it took him a moment to register the stunned faces in the foyer.

"Has something happened?" he eventually asked.

"Not really," groaned Mojo, who was being helped to his feet by Jake. "Lindsey was just showing me what a good loser she is, that's all. Nothing serious."

Puzzlement and concern briefly crossed Adrian Brand's face, but didn't stay long. "Well, I'm afraid that's where you're wrong," he exclaimed, suddenly remembering why he was there. "Something extremely serious has happened."

149

Phil Hammond was now walking towards the *Post* stall, just like everyone else in the foyer. "What is it?" he asked.

"This," replied Adrian Brand, pulling a copy of Jake and Mojo's newspaper from his pocket and tapping the front page ominously. "I've just shown it to the head. I demanded to know if it was true, but he wouldn't say. He just went red in the face and started shouting at me."

Jake and Mojo looked at each other while Phil folded his arms. "Did he?"

"Yes," confirmed Adrian. "And what's more he wants to see all three of you – Shepherd, Johnson and you too, Philip, in his office. Right away."

Sitting on a bench outside Tom Busby's office, Jake and Mojo could still hear the sound of muffled voices twenty minutes after Phil Hammond had gone in.

"What do you think he's going to do?" asked Jake.

"Who?"

"Busby."

"Nothing," replied Mojo. He paused to examine the bruise on his left ankle for signs of growth, then continued. "What can he do? He'll just give us a bollocking for leaking about the staff cuts, that's all."

"Yeah." Jake looked reassured. "You're right." He leaned back. There was a brief pause, then he leaned forward again. "You don't think Hammond's going to get into trouble, though – for letting us print it, I mean?"

Mojo gave a world-weary sigh. "Will you relax? All we have to say is Hammond didn't know anything about it."

"Which is true."

"Which is true. So stop getting your knickers in a twist."

"I'm not!" Jake crossed his legs and tried to look calm, but his left knee jiggled nervously.

"Just think of Woodward and Bernstein," said Mojo.

"Who?"

"The blokes who found out about Watergate. God, you're ignorant, you are."

"Me!" Jake pointed a finger at his own chest.

"Yeah, you. Fancy not know— " Before Mojo could say any more, Tom Busby's door opened and the headmaster himself looked into the corridor.

"Right you two – come on in," he said, and retreated again, leaving the door open. Slowly Jake and Mojo got up, solemnly shook hands with each other, then went in.

A shaft of bright sunshine was pouring through the office window and for a moment Jake was dazzled by it. Then his eyes adjusted and he noticed that Barry Crane was in the room as well as Phil Hammond and Tom Busby. All three of them looked extremely sombre, especially Barry Crane. "Sit down," said Tom, indicating two chairs directly in front of his desk. Jake and Mojo sat down. "Now then," the headmaster began, "I gather you two are responsible for this." He held up a copy of the *Post*.

"Yes, sir," said Jake softly.

"What's that? Speak up, boy."

"I said 'Yes, sir'."

"Right. And I also gather you've just enterprisingly sold 200 copies of it."

"190, sir," corrected Mojo. "You see we kept one back for Mr Hammond and one each for ourselves, and on top of . . ."

Tom Busby fixed Mojo with a gimlet-eyed stare, then continued. "In other words, over thirty percent of the students in this school have bought the *Portobello Post* and read this 'staff cuts' nonsense," he jabbed the front page with his forefinger.

Jake swallowed. "Nonsense, sir?"

"Yes, 'nonsense'," Tom Busby repeated. "Because there aren't going to *be* any staff cuts. None. Do I

151

make myself clear?" There was a short, tense silence. "So what you've printed isn't a daring exposé or a scoop or whatever else you may have thought it was – it's just an unfounded, irresponsible rumour!" At this point he threw the *Post* angrily onto his desk for emphasis. "And I am very upset about it."

"But the report— " Mojo protested weakly.

"That report," the headmaster continued, growing steadily redder in the face, "Mr Crane's report," he indicated his deputy with a gesture of the right hand, "the confidential report you quote in your *article* was in point of fact a set of recommendations which I rejected two weeks ago. Since then, at a lengthy financial planning session with the governors and the local education authority we agreed to cut costs in other areas."

"Oh," said Jake.

"Oh," repeated Tom Busby. "You didn't know about that, did you? And why? Because you didn't bother to check your facts or talk to anybody, that's why. Oh no, you just stole a confidential report, drew your own assumptions and then, without a by-your-leave, without . . . without even consulting Mr *Hammond*," this time his indicating hand went out to the left, "you printed a completely false story damaging to staff morale." Breathing heavily he leaned forward so that his knuckles turned white against the desk top. "What have you got to say for yourselves?"

Jake glanced at Phil Hammond who was shifting uneasily in his chair. "Well we didn't actually steal the report," he explained. "We just, sort of, saw it one day in Mrs Mogridge's office when she wasn't there – that's all." Barry Crane, nostrils quivering with outrage, was gripping both arms of his chair.

"And we couldn't check out the story, could we?" said Mojo, addressing Tom Busby and taking up Jake's explanation. "I mean, even if it had been true, you'd only have denied it or shut us up or something. *We* didn't know it was just whaddycallem . . . 'recommendations'. We just thought we'd found out something really important the kids in this school should know about."

"Yeah," Jake agreed. "And that was the whole point of the *Post* – to get *real* news stories." He looked at Barry Crane, then Tom Busby and finally Phil Hammond. "We didn't mean it to turn out like this, did we, Mo?"

"No."

"Honest."

"Yeah," Mojo nodded soberly. "Honest."

Except for the ticking of an imitation ormolu clock the room then fell completely silent for ten seconds until Tom Busby finally said in a calm, very still voice, "But it has turned out like this, and I'm afraid you must be punished."

"Headmaster," interrupted Phil Hammond. "I'm sure there must be some other . . ."

"Mr Hammond, if – you – *don't* – mind," said Tom Busby emphatically. He waited to make absolutely sure that Phil had stopped speaking, then returned his attention to Jake and Mojo. "You will both report to me here at 9 o'clock tomorrow morning when I will tell you what I intend to do about this matter. Understood?"

"Yes, sir," mumbled the two boys in unison.

"Right – you may go."

Outside, Jake and Mojo walked down the corridor in complete silence. Only when they were safely out of earshot round a corner did Mojo give vent to his anger. "It's a bloody cover up," he fumed, kicking a piece of loose skirting board. He glowered at the wall for a moment, then wheeled round and grabbed a fistful of Jake's baseball jacket. "Isn't it?"

Jake put a hand on his friend's shoulder. "Take it easy," he said. "Look – we made a mistake, OK. Face facts – we were wrong."

"But we *weren't*!" Mojo insisted, blinking several times.

153

"Isn't it obvious? There are still going to be staff cuts, only now we've blown the whistle Busby's denying it 'cos he can't afford to admit the *Post* was right." He snorted derisively. " 'We had to cut costs in other areas.' Hah! £90,000 a year? *You* saw the figures in Crane's report. How's he going to save that 'in other areas'? Oh no —" Mojo's expression became even more serious as he wagged a finger in Jake's face. "Oh no – you wait. He's still going to sack people."

Jake gently pushed the finger away. "Maybe – maybe not," he said, sounding distant and preoccupied. "But to be honest it's not the teachers I'm worried about at the moment." He took a deep breath and let it go. "Right now I reckon the people most likely to get the sack are you and me."

Chapter 10

Dear Kyle,

Hi, babycakes. God, it was great talking to you last week – I am *so* glad you're finally out of the hospital. One thing, though – this "Kathleen Turner look-a-like" physiotherapist who's coming to the house every day – just tell her *no funny business,* OK? (joke).

Lauren looked up from the airmail pad balanced on her knees. What next? She reached across the bed and slotted a Bruce Hornsby cassette into the tape machine. The hotel? The hearing? What had happened to Jake and Mojo? She chewed the end of her Biro pensively. OK, start with the hotel.

"Lots of news. First, I booked a place for you to stay when you come over in February. It's a really neat little hotel just a few blocks from here called "The Lord Raglan" – how British can you get, right? Anyway, its got horse brasses in the lobby and the couple who run the place are straight out of P. G. Wodehouse – you'll love it.

The only possible fly in the ointment is Antony Cormack's trial. Right now nobody seems to know when it's going to be, but there's a preliminary hearing next week, so maybe we'll find out then. Meanwhile, things round here are still kinda tense, and Gudrun (Charlie's Mom) is getting more and more hyper by the hour. You can see why, though – like, how *do* you react when your husband's about to go on trial and the whole thing's being dragged through the newspapers? In some weird way it's not so bad for Antony himself – he's super-busy preparing the case and that keeps his mind occupied. Anyway, waiting's always the hardest part – that's what they say, isn't it? – so maybe the situation will look a little brighter on Monday. I'll keep you posted."

Yeah, but maybe it wouldn't. Tapping the end of her pen on the bed, Lauren sighed. What if Antony really was guilty? What if he went to jail? For a minute she sat completely still in the lamplit attic room. Then, softly murmuring "Come on, come on," she stretched, shook out her arms like an athlete before a race and began writing again.

"Talking of the press, we had a little scandal at Portobello a few days ago. Remember I told you about this Media Studies project that's been going on with the rival newspapers? – well, last Friday was the big launch where they tried to outsell each other. Jake and Mojo (they're the guys I'm in the band with) won – or they sold the most copies at any rate – but then it all backfired because they printed this front page story about a plan to cut staff at the school but it turned out they'd got the whole thing wrong. Boy, did the you-know-what hit the fan! Some of the kids even thought they might be expelled, but in the end what happened was they just had to hand over the money they'd made (around $50) as 'libel damages'. Humiliating, but I guess it could have been worse. Oh yeah, they had to put up a big apology on the school noticeboard, too. Anyhow, it all turned out OK because the money's going towards a fund that's been set up to buy new video equipment for the Media Studies department, so I guess . . ."

Just then there was a loud, insistent rapping on the trap door. Lauren paused, pen in hand, and glanced up. "Come in."

It was Charlie's face that appeared, pale and anxious, as the door banged open. For a moment she appeared unable to speak and just stood on the top rung of the ladder gasping for breath. Then, her jaw quivering, she said: "It's over."

Lauren looked at her. "What's over? Charlie, are you OK?"

"He's killed himself."

Lauren made a small whimpering sound and put a hand to her mouth. "Oh my God! Your father's . . ."

"No, not Dad." Charlie paused to catch her breath. "The man who was really behind the whole Strelson thing. It's just been on the start of the Nine O'Clock News. He took an overdose."

"Who? Charlie, *who* took an overdose? You're not making any sense."

"Piers Matheson – he was a director at Mercantile Finance. They found his body in a hotel room in Geneva a few hours ago. He'd left a full written confession."

Lauren couldn't believe her ears. "A confession!"

"Yes. That's all they said in the headlines, but there'll be more later in the programme. Look, you'd better come downstairs."

"I'll be right there."

As Charlie disappeared from view Lauren jumped off the bed. Then, pausing only to pull on a pair of trainers and mutter "My *God*", she followed her down the stepladder.

In the Cormacks' living room, Gudrun was perched on the edge of an enormous cream sofa watching the TV news as Charlie and Lauren ran into the room.

"Where's Dad?" asked Charlie, sitting next to her mother.

"In his study," Gudrun replied, not taking her eyes off the screen. "He's calling Sir Patrick to find out if . . . wait, this is it." She half-turned. "ANTONY!" A few moments later Antony Cormack appeared in the doorway just as the newsreader handed over to a stern, raincoated correspondent in Geneva. It was snowing and behind her a small crowd had gathered on the steps of a floodlit hotel. Realizing the cameras were rolling, she began to speak.

"Staff here at the Hotel de la Paix found the body of 47-year-old Mr Piers Matheson earlier this evening. Initial reports suggest that Mr Matheson, a director of the troubled Mercantile Finance group, took his own life. Beside his bed in the locked room was an empty bottle of powerful tranquillisers and a suicide note. In the note Mr Matheson confessed to being responsible for irregular share-dealings concerning the takeover of Strelson Electronics by Intertel Communications, one of America's leading multinational companies. Six weeks ago police arrested another of Mercantile's directors, Mr Antony Cormack, on insider-dealing charges related to the takeover, but that case now seems likely to be either dropped or at least delayed pending further investigations after today's events. This is Kate Lawson for the Nine O'Clock News in Geneva."

Reaching forward from his armchair, Antony Cormack switched off the set by remote control. Then, his face totally drained of emotion, he sat back. Gudrun glanced across the room, her hands twisting in her lap.

"What did Patrick say?"

Antony massaged his eyebrows with thumb and forefinger before replying. "He says he's talked to the police and apparently Matheson's confession puts me completely in the clear. There's going to be a board meeting in the morning and obviously they'll have to set up an inquiry and so forth, but . . ." he took a deep, juddering breath ". . . well, after that it looks like the whole bloody nightmare will be over."

A smile fluttered across Gudrun's face. "Over?" she repeated, as if she couldn't quite grasp what he'd said.

"Yes. Over." Antony Cormack stood up, moved across to the sofa and put an arm gently round his wife's shoulders. They looked at each other, Gudrun's eyes slowly filling with tears.

"Oh, Tony," she whispered. "I'm so . . ." then, convulsed by a sudden spasm of release, she rushed both hands to her face and began to sob uncontrollably.

"And you really liked it – you're not just saying that?" Jake slurped a mouthful of coffee and looked anxiously across the living room at 64 Antrobus Road.

"Yes." Kay turned to Graham who was beside her on the sofa. "He just won't believe us, will he?"

"Apparently not."

"Well, it wasn't as good as usual, that's why," Jake explained. "Normally it's not such a rowdy crowd, and then I went and fluffed one of the solos near the beginni . . ."

"*Jake!*" Kay put down her mug. "Stop telling us how awful it was. Look – Graham and I may be over 35, we may not listen to live pop music in pubs very often and we may not be the best judges of what we heard today, but nevertheless we thought you, Maurice and Lauren were wonderful, all right?" There was no answer so she reached over and shook his knee. "All right?"

"Yeah, all right." Jake grinned sheepishly. "If you say so." The conversation moved onto other topics after that – a film Graham and Kay had seen the previous night – cars – the progress of the local police football team. Jake listened politely for a while, then collected the coffee mugs together and got to his feet. "I'll wash up," he said.

A few minutes later Kay followed him into the kitchen where she leaned against the draining board and lit a cheroot. Jake carried on with what he was doing. "There's

159

at least two days' worth here," he murmured, indicating a stack of encrusted pans, plates and cutlery on the worktop to his right. Kay stared at the dishes with an air of mild disgust.

"Mmmm, well that's nothing new, is it?" There was a lengthy pause before Jake spoke again.

"So did you talk to him about Cornwall?"

Silence.

"Mum?"

"I know, I know – don't bully me." Kay ran one hand morosely up and down the arm of her green mohair sweater. "I will – I just haven't found the right moment yet." She made a face at the kitchen table. "God, that sounds really pathetic, doesn't it?"

"No . . . but . . ."

"You see, it's not just Cornwall," Kay interrupted, a look of quiet desperation crossing her face. "It's more than that."

"How do you mean?"

"Well, everything's happening at once – the exhibition, Graham . . . I just . . . I don't know . . . I need some time to sort it all out."

Jake reached for a teatowel off the three-pronged rack beside the cooker and began drying his hands. "So what are you saying – you want to postpone the wedding?"

"I think so." Kay gnawed her bottom lip and sighed. "Or do I? Several seconds passed, then she tapped her forehead gently with an index finger. "Oh, I don't know what I want."

"Look . . ," Jake began. Just then the opening bars of a Beethoven string quartet came from the living room. "Ah, *real* music," he remarked, as they both smiled. "Told you he didn't like pop."

"People can like both. Go on – what were you going to say?"

"Oh yeah. Well . . ." Jake rubbed his nose with the back of a damp forearm. ". . . I was planning to go to

160

the pool in a while, so why don't the two of you have a chat then? Be the perfect opportunity."

Kay stared at him, visibly thinking. "OK," she said in the end.

"You mean it?"

"Yes." She inhaled with determination. "You're right. I've been putting it off and off. Honestly, though, I just . . ."

"I know, Mum. You just need a bit of time. So *tell* him – it's not the end of the world. He'll wait – I'm sure he will."

Kay smiled, then put the flat of one hand on her stomach to stop a sudden attack of nerves. "I'll finish up here," she said after the moment had passed. "Why don't you go through?"

"Fine." Jake got to the door and turned round. "Oh, and Mum?"

"Yes?" Kay looked over one shoulder.

"Good luck."

Back in the living room Graham was sitting in a shaft of watery December sunlight and making small conducting gestures with his right hand. Jake sat down opposite him and they both smiled amiably. "So." The hand stopped conducting. "All done?"

"Not quite." Jake rolled down his sleeves. "Mum's drying up. She'll be a few minutes yet."

"Ahhh." Graham stood up, moved to the door and gently closed it. Then he returned to his chair and sat down again. "In that case I think you and I should have a quiet word."

"You and me?"

"Yes."

"What about?"

Jake changed position, groaning inwardly. Oh God, why now? He hadn't mentioned Cornwall all week. Why, just at the very moment when . . . "This." Reaching into

Kay's bag beside the sofa, Graham pulled out a copy of the *Portobello Post*.

"Oh."

"Your Mum showed it to me yesterday and . . . well, there's something in it I wanted to talk to you about."

"Right." Jake felt the colour draining from his face as Graham turned to the article on Paul Leary and held it up. "Two of my officers arrested this man last night."

"*Arrested* him? But . . . what for?"

The muscles in Graham's jaw tightened. "Selling heroin."

"*What?*"

"I'm afraid so. He was a dealer – one of the biggest on the local housing estates. We've been watching him for weeks."

"But . . ." Jake was lost for words. He looked at the photograph now hanging limply across the arm of Graham's chair. "But, what about how he got beaten up? I talked to his mates. They were there. They were *witnesses*."

Graham nodded gravely. "Did he tell you the name of the officer who beat him up?"

For a moment Jake hesitated, then went on. There was nothing left to lose. "Yeah – Downing. He said one of them was called Downing."

"Ahhh."

"But we didn't put it in the article 'cos we couldn't actually prove it."

"Well, you were absolutely right not to," said Graham. "Because you see that's exactly what he wanted. He knew that Sergeant Downing was onto him – I imagine he was just using your paper to try and get him pulled off the case."

A combination of anger and puzzlement mingled in Jake's face. "Yeah, but . . ."

"How did Leary get beaten up? We arrested him with another dealer – one of your 'witnesses' – and he gave

162

us the whole story." Graham linked his fingers. "What happened is this. About a month ago two of Leary's customers roughed him up when his prices got a little high for their liking. Well, Leary simply convinced a group of friends to go along with his police harassment story hoping they could use it against Bill Downing. It's as simple as that."

Stunned, Jake gazed at his feet. "And we bought the whole thing."

"Correction, you nearly bought the whole thing." Graham leaned forward, pointing an emphatic finger. "Which, I might add, is all that saved you from getting one of my men into very serious trouble." He fixed his deep-set grey eyes on Jake for what seemed like an interminable length of time, then sat back again. "As it is," he put the *Post* back into Kay's bag with an air of grim satisfaction, "we've got him on a watertight charge and he'll be going away for a very long time."

"I can't believe it." Jake exhaled unevenly and put both hands to his head.

"I thought you should know," said Graham.

"Yeah."

"For your own good."

"Yeah." Jake nodded. "Thanks."

"That's all right." Graham stood up. "We all make mistakes." He patted Jake on the shoulder, took a deep breath and moved towards the door. "Now – I wonder how that mother of yours is getting on in the kitchen."

Half an hour later Jake was on his twentieth length at the Kensington New Pools. Breathing every three strokes, kicking rhythmically, tumble-turning, pushing off, surfacing – his body was on automatic pilot and had been from about the fifth length. As usual when he swam though, Jake's mind was on anything *but* automatic pilot. For some reason he always did his best thinking in the pool and today there was certainly plenty to think about.

Paul Leary, his mother and Graham, the aftermath of the *Post*, the future of Nexus, the news about Charlie Cormack's Dad, even Charlie Cormack herself, come to that . . . Slowly Jake sifted through them all as he swam up and down. Eventually though he kept coming back to Charlie. Somehow no matter how hard he tried to focus on anything else her face kept appearing, or if not her face, her voice or the sound of her laughing or some detail like the way she had of pushing a strand of hair behind one ear. Why? Why should he be thinking about *her* of all people when there were so many other things going on – really important things to think about? It didn't make any sense.

Disconcerted, Jake swam on, determined to finish the forty lengths he'd set himself, but in the end he cheated and stopped after thirty-six. Standing up in the shallow end he breathed hard for a minute, then hauled himself into a sitting position on the side of the pool, feet and calves still in the water. "I couldn't be," he told himself. "No, that's ridiculous. I just couldn't be." He pulled off his goggles and frowned at the rippling, glinting water below him. "Could I?"

"Right, can I have some hush, please? Jake – headphones off, if you don't mind." Phil Hammond sat on his desk and faced the class. "Thank you. Now, as I'm sure nobody here needs reminding, this is our last lesson together before the Christmas holidays. Ahhhh. Yes, I know." He grinned. "But I still want to finish yesterday's discussion on what we've done this term, OK?" There was a moment's general throat-clearing and chair-shuffling. "Good." Phil reached behind him and picked up a copy of the *Portobello Gazette*. "Well, we've already talked about Lauren and Dave's report on new technology and the version of twenty-first century journalism predicted by Aftab and Brendan, so today . . ." he held up the *Gazette*

164

". . . I want to start with Charlotte and Lindsey's project." The two girls darted a rapid glance at each other while Phil leafed through the paper.

"The first thing I noticed about this is how professionally it's put together. All the technical skills are there, and the standard in everything from photo-cropping to writing headlines, layout, typography . . . is all excellent."

"Good photo of you and all, sir," Aftab interjected. Phil allowed himself a wry smile and pressed on. "As for the editorial side – well, there's quite a broad mix, and several of the articles – I'm thinking particularly of the drug rehabilitation feature and . . . what was the other one? . . . oh yes, the piece you had on local employment schemes – were balanced and very well written indeed. However . . ." he looked up and rubbed the back of his neck, "there were a few others that weren't so well balanced. The feature on race relations, for example. I mean, girls, I know the point of the *Gazette* was to be positive, but honestly, to read this you'd think there was hardly a race problem in London at all!"

Lindsey folded her arms and leaned forward. "Well, there shouldn't be."

"Fine. I agree. But that's an editorial opinion, not news."

Lindsey sat back looking only half-convinced.

"Anyway, all in all there's a great deal to admire in the *Gazette* and apart from the odd lapse into wishful thinking instead of journalism, I'd say it's a fine piece of work. Well done." As a low-key round of applause went up, Charlie acknowledged it with a jokingly regal wave of the hand while Lindsey, still slightly miffed, contented herself with a brief bob of the head.

"Which brings me to the *Portobello Post*." An expectant hush fell over the room as Phil produced a copy of Jake and Mojo's newspaper. "Now we all know what happened last week" – he paused while a ripple of laughter dispelled – "but setting that aside for a moment if we may, there

165

are a few overall journalistic comments I'd like to make."
Mojo winced in anticipation. "To begin with the *Post* is
written in good, clear English, which is more than certain
so-called 'professional' tabloids can claim." More laughter. "Plus which from the standpoint of photos, captions,
design and so on, it's all very well presented – not as glossy
and upmarket as . . . well, let's just say 'another newspaper I could mention', but still well presented. All right,
all right. Thank you. Settle down. And as for the content
– well, it's newsworthy, entertaining and in some cases
almost uncomfortably relevant – BUT — " Phil raised
a warning finger just as a relieved Jake and Mojo were
about to shake hands under the desk, " — good journalism isn't just about clear English, good presentation and
being relevant; important though all those things are, it's
primarily about getting the *facts* right." He addressed this
remark directly to Jake and Mojo, remaining motionless
just long enough to make sure it had sunk in, then lifted
a significant eyebrow and replaced the *Post* on his desk.

Meanwhile Lindsey turned to Charlie. "Wasn't 'honest'
missing from that list?" she muttered.

"OK, now as I said yesterday I'll be handing out
assessment grades and talking to all of you individually
before term ends on Thursday . . ." Phil got up and
shucked off his leather jacket ". . . but since this is our
last pre-festive session as a group, I think we should spend
the rest of it talking about what we'll be doing in January,
don't you?"

"Rock'n'*rolllll*," Mojo called out from the back.

"Pithy as ever, Maurice," Phil agreed. "But it won't
just be rock and roll – it's everything to do with the 'sound'
media – that's radio, too. And remember, even if your
project *is* on the music industry, there are other styles
of music apart from rock and pop. Jazz, for instance, or
country, world music . . . even opera."

"*Opera!*" Dave looked astounded.

Phil cast his eyes up to the ceiling. "All right, all

right – maybe not opera, but you get the general idea."

"Sir, could we tape a radio programme for one of the local stations?" asked Charlie enthusiastically.

"Or write something about how record companies work?" chipped in Aftab.

"Fine." Phil spread his arms. "As long as it's connected with some aspect of what we'll be covering in the coursework."

Other suggestions were put forward and a general discussion began. Meanwhile, in the back row, Jake leaned across to Mojo. "Do you reckon us getting national airplay for the first Nexus single would count?" he asked.

Mojo twisted his mouth to one side and thought about it. "Could do," he replied, giving the possibility serious consideration. It obviously appealed, because after a second he broke into a broad grin. "In fact, come to think of it . . . that could do very nicely indeed."

Epilogue

"Can I give you a refill, Mrs Mogridge? I'm doing the rounds."

"That's very kind of you, Headmaster." Angela Mogridge held out an empty plastic cup which Tom Busby filled from a bottle of Chianti. "Thanks."

Phil Hammond and Cora Peters walked by, followed by Aftab, Lindsey and Dave. "Quite a good do this year, don't you think?" asked Tom, nodding to Vic Drake and Barry Crane as he surveyed the packed main hall.

"Yes." Angela coughed twice to clear a frog in her throat. "I was just saying to Mr Brand how nice the decorations looked."

Tom Busby brought his head a little closer. "Tell me – what did you think of the live entertainment just now? What is it they call themselves? – 'Nexus'?"

"That's right," replied Angela.

"Not your sort of thing, I'd imagine."

"No, not really," Angela confessed, sotto voce, "but I have to admit they're very good. Very professional." She placed a hand to the neck of her blue, crêpe-de-chine dress and fiddled with a string of imitation pearls. "Don't you agree?" she said, head to one side.

On the other side of the hall Jake and Lauren were sitting on the stage, deep in conversation. Mojo had gone off to the bar. "OK, so you're saying the 17th, 18th and 19th – is that it?" asked Lauren, flicking through her diary.

"Yeah – from ten in the morning to six. I gave you the address, didn't I?"

"Wait – I know it's here someplace – yeah, 'Reel

Recording, 302 Tredenham Mews, SW9'. Fine." She wrote down the dates, then snapped her diary shut with one hand and grinned. "Can't wait."

"Me neither." Jake ran the fingers of one hand adroitly through his blond cowlick. "Especially if we play like we did tonight."

"Whoa, Mr Modesty!" Lauren laughed, adding, "Mind you, we were kinda good, I have to say. And did you see Cora Peters and Adrian Brand actually *dancing* during the last number?"

"I know." Jake looked amazed. "Unbelievable, eh?"

They both chuckled, acknowledging the evening's success, then Lauren gazed thoughtfully round the crowded room, cupping her chin in both hands. "In fact, come to think of it, the last couple of *months* have been pretty unbelievable," she murmured.

"Yeah, I know what you mean." Jake glanced at the floor for a second then looked up. "What's the latest on Charlie's Dad, by the way?"

"Well, he's still waiting to get the all-clear, but it looks pretty good. They're saying he should be able to go back to work after the vacation."

"That soon!"

"Mm."

"Great!" Jake beamed. "God, he must be so relieved."

Lauren greeted this with wry laughter. "Let me tell you he is *not* the only one. Anyhow . . ." she straightened her back ". . . that's all over. Now all I want to do is get into the recording studio and then head off for ten days of sun and snow."

She saw surprise register on Jake's face. "Oh, didn't you know? I'm going skiing in Austria with Charlie and her folks over Christmas and New Year's."

"Skiing?"

"Yeah, 'skiing'. You put these long pieces of wood on your . . ."

"Lauren!" Jake grinned. "No, I didn't know."

"Oh. Well, I am. It was Charlie's idea as a matter of fact. Neat, huh?"

Jake nodded. "By the way," he began in a slightly constricted tone of voice, ". . . is Charlie coming tonight? I haven't seen her." Lauren was gazing round to see where Mojo had got to with the drinks.

"Yeah," she replied.

"Oh, good."

Something about that "Oh, good" made Lauren stop looking for Mojo and turn her attention to Jake. "Why?" she asked, suddenly suspicious. "You and Mojo don't have some little end-of-term prank up your sleeves, do you?"

"No."

"Are you sure? Because if you do, I just think you should— "

"Lauren."

"What?"

"You've got it all wrong."

Bemused, Lauren stopped in mid-flow. "I have?" She frowned.

"Yes."

"What? What have I got wrong?"

"Me and Charlie. I don't want to wind her up." Jake paused, smiling. "Just the opposite, actually."

"Wait, wait, wait. Back up a minute – I'm not sure I'm following this conversation. What exactly are you talking about?"

"Well . . ." Jake took a deep breath. "I suppose you might as well know. I've decided to ask her ou—"

"LAUREN! There you are! We've been looking everywhere. God, I'm sorry we're so late, but Julian's train was held up. Never mind, we're here . . . now." Appearing out of the crowd beside the dance floor, Charlie suddenly stopped as she realized who Lauren was with. "Oh . . . hello."

Jake raised one arm in an awkward gesture. "Hi."

After a momentary pause, Charlie produced a bright smile which didn't quite reach her eyes and turned abruptly to the man standing behind her – a slim, patrician-looking aesthete with startlingly blue eyes, floppy fair hair and high cheekbones. "Julian – this is Lauren," she said.

The man leaned forwards to shake hands, his pale blue eyes glinting amiably. "How do you do? Charlotte has told me so much about you."

Lauren returned the handshake. "Ditto." The pale blue eyes looked puzzled. "I mean, she's told me a lot about you, too."

"Ahh – of course."

"And this is Jake Shepherd. Jake . . . Julian Goss."

"Now I don't think I've heard about *you*." Julian smiled and extended his hand again. "Never mind – pleased to meet you."

"Hi," replied Jake, receiving a limp bundle of fingers.

"Well . . ." Charlie looked round, taking in the packed hall in one circular gaze. "This place certainly looks different from normal, doesn't it?" Her smile slipped for a fraction of a second in the ensuing silence, then Lauren came to the rescue.

"Mmmmm – certainly does."

Jake turned to Julian. "So – uh – how's the rugby? Having a good season?"

"Sorry?"

Jake looked perplexed. "I thought Charlie said you played rugby."

Now it was Julian's turn to be perplexed. "Hardly! Can't stand the game. No, I'm afraid chess is the most strenuous sport I ever play." He emitted a short braying laugh.

"Ah." Jake glanced towards Charlie and gave her a sweet smile. "I must have got it wrong."

"Yes, you must," she replied curtly.

"I love your dress, Charlie," said Lauren hurriedly.

171

"It looks brand new. Is that the one you bought in Knightsbridge last week?"

Charlie opened her mouth to reply, but before she could, Mojo arrived and began distributing drinks to Jake and Lauren. "Right – here we go – oh, hi, Charlie, didn't see you there – sorry about the wait, chaps – anyway, better late than never, eh? Cheers." He took a mouthful from his own cup, beamed enthusiastically at everyone else, and finally spotted Julian. "Who's this then?"

Charlie sighed. "Maurice – this is Julian, a friend of mine from Oxford who's down for the weekend."

"Oh, right." Mojo nodded to Julian. "That makes me feel better."

"Really?" Julian smiled weakly, raising his voice as a particularly loud dance track started booming out of the speakers behind them on stage. "Why's that?"

"Because I brought a couple of friends along, too," replied Mojo, "and I wasn't sure if it was kosher or not."

"Was one of them Alex?" asked Lauren. "I thought I saw her just a minute ago."

"Yeah." Mojo took another mouthful of wine, boogying on the spot, his eyes roving the crowd. "And the other one's . . . where is she?" He pointed, ". . . there!"

Jake followed his finger. "The girl dancing with Brendan?" He looked, looked away, then did a double-take, choking on a mouthful of wine in the process. "But isn't that . . . ?"

Mojo nodded. "Desirée Montgomery? Absolutely."

Lauren covered her eyes. "Oh brother."

"But does Brendan know she's . . ." Jake was unable to finish the sentence because he'd now started to laugh and choke at the same time.

" 'Course not!" replied Mojo. "I told him she was called Joyce – which is true, actually. Desirée's just her stage name." He smiled. "Sweet, isn't it? – they seem to be getting on like a house on fire. Jake? You all right?"

Jake was now red in the face and coughing into

his right hand. "Hang on, I know what to do," said Mojo, rolling up one sleeve and wiggling his eyebrows confidently at Lauren. He then gave Jake a hefty slap between the shoulder blades which stopped him coughing immediately but also shot most of his wine all over the front of Charlie's dress. For a long, pained moment she just stared in silence at the ugly, red stain. Then, slowly raising her head, she glowered furiously at Jake.

"I didn't . . ." he began feebly, but it was too late. Charlie had already grasped Julian by the hand and was steering him off towards the dance floor.

"Nice going, guys," said Lauren appreciatively as the remaining trio watched them leave. "Really nice going." There was a short pause before she turned, folded her arms and added: "Promise me something."

"What?" asked Mojo.

"Just promise me next term won't be like this one."

Jake sighed. "Wish I could . . ." He narrowed his eyes and looked upwards, as if the future was somewhere to be found among the flashing lights. "But d'you know something, Lauren? One way or another I don't think I can."

Stevie Day
Series

JACQUELINE WILSON

Supersleuth	£2.25	☐
Lonely Hearts	£2.25	☐
Rat Race	£2.25	☐
Vampire	£2.25	☐

An original new series featuring an unlikely but irresistible heroine – fourteen-year-old Stevie Day, a small skinny feminist who has a good eye for detail which, combined with a wild imagination, helps her solve mysteries.

"Jacqueline Wilson is a skilful writer, readers of ten and over will find the (Stevie Day) books good, light-hearted entertainment."

Children's Books December 1987

"Sparky Stevie" *T.E.S. January 1988*

ARMADA

Run With the Hare

LINDA NEWBERY

A sensitive and authentic novel exploring the workings of an animal rights group, through the eyes of Elaine, a sixth-form pupil. Elaine becomes involved with the group through her more forceful friend Kate, and soon becomes involved with Mark, an Adult Education student and one of the more sophisticated members of the group. Elaine finds herself painting slogans and sabotaging a fox hunt. Then she and her friends uncover a dog fighting ring – and things turn very nasty.

£1.95   □

Hairline Cracks

JOHN ROBERT TAYLOR

A gritty, tense and fast-paced story of kidnapping, fraud and cover ups. Sam Lydney's mother knows too much. She's realized that a public inquiry into the safety of a nuclear power station has been rigged. Now she's disappeared and Sam's sure she has been kidnapped, he can trust no one except his resourceful friend Mo, and together they are determined to uncover the crooks' operation and, more importantly, find Sam's mother.

£1.95   □

ARMADA

All these books are available at your local bookshop or newsagent, or can be ordered from the publisher. To order direct from the publishers just tick the title you want and fill in the form below:

Name _____

Address _____

_____

Send to: Collins Childrens Cash Sales
         PO Box 11
         Falmouth
         Cornwall
         TR10 9EN

Please enclose a cheque or postal order or debit my Visa/ Access –

   Credit card no:

   Expiry date:

   Signature:

– to the value of the cover price plus:

UK: 60p for the first book, 25p for the second book, plus 15p per copy for each additional book ordered to a maximum charge of £1.90.

BFPO: 60p for the first book, 25p for the second book plus 15p per copy for the next 7 books, thereafter 9p per book.

Overseas and Eire: £1.25 for the first book, 75p for the second book. Thereafter 28p per book.

ARMADA